FEED

MICHAEL BRAY

SEVERED PRESS
HOBART TASMANIA

FEED

PART ONE

CHAPTER ONE

Tyler Matthews looked at the woman standing at the entrance to his apartment and rcaliscd shc was a stranger. She looked and sounded almost the same as the woman he had fallen in love with seven years earlier, but the edges were harder on this iteration, the eyes harsh, lips without a smile and turned into a disapproving sneer. This version of Amy was an impostor, a cold thing in an Amy mask.

'You realise this will be it, don't you? Our marriage will be over if you do this.' The impostor Amy crossed her arms to emphasise the point, one of her many bad habits that he had grown to detest.

'Yeah, I know that,' Tyler said, and it was true. He knew it was over and didn't care. It had been a while since he had felt anything that could have been taken for love. First, there was frustration and tolerance which, over time, had grown into bitter indifference and longing to be free of the shackles he had married into.

'And you're going to do it anyway? What the hell is wrong with you? Don't you even want to fight for this? For us?'

He sighed and stared at his bare feet, curling his toes in the carpet, wondering if he should invite her in then deciding against it. 'I don't want to get into this again. We both know this is for the best. The sooner you come to terms with it, the better.'

'Best for you. Not best for me. There's a difference and you know it.'

A few years ago, a comment like that would have sparked a furious and passionate argument which would culminate in spectacular make-up sex later. Not anymore, though; now there was no room for desire. Only hatred. He badly wanted her to go away and leave him alone and wondered why she had come over. He had made it clear enough that whatever they once had was over, and yet she was stubborn in her refusal to play along. Her presence was putting a black cloud over his day, the negative energy hanging thick and heavy over the threshold to the house. 'You chose to leave, Amy. Not me. You went and decided to move in with Tim.'

She flinched and looked away. 'You forced me into that. I'd tried to keep us going by myself for so long and couldn't do it anymore. Tim was there for me when you weren't. He was there when I needed somebody. I realise now it was a mistake. I've changed my mind.'

He shook his head and flashed her a cynical grin. 'That makes it alright then. You decide the affair wasn't going to grow into something more like you hoped it would then think it's okay to come back because you changed your mind. I'm done letting you walk all over me. Things have changed.'

'You drove me to it.'

'Don't try to put this on me. I stuck to the vows of our marriage.' He hated that she was getting him angry. He'd promised himself he wouldn't let that happen and hated her a little bit more for it.

'Don't you dare try to claim this was all one sided. You neglected me. You forced me to look elsewhere. This is as much your fault as it is mine.'

She had a point. He *had* neglected her. He had grown bored and started to feel trapped by the cocoon she had built. Steady and unspectacular job. A circle of friends who he had nothing in common with as they were mostly hers (especially Tim. She knew

Tim really well). He had been manipulated into a boring existence, a cycle of meaningless days melting into each other which she expected him to do for the rest of his life. 'Yeah, well, I suppose we're both to blame,' he muttered, wishing there was an easier way to do things like this.

Amy was frustrated and angry; he could see it in the way her lip curled down at the corner. 'Jesus, Tyler, you mean to go through with this, don't you?'

Typical Amy. Thinking the world revolved around her and never expecting that someone else might have plans that didn't involve her. 'Yeah,' he said again, keeping with the answer that had served him well so far.

'You know it's insane, right? Giving up your job, a good job, a well-paid job. Selling the house to move into this shitty apartment.'

'The apartment is temporary. It's better that walking around that tomb of a house and being constantly reminded of you and what happened. And for the record, I *hated* that job.'

'My brother got you that job, you ungrateful asshole.'

'Exactly. *You* chose it. *You* asked your brother to put the word in without asking how I felt. *You* bullied me into taking it even though I didn't want to. That was never my job, it was yours. I was just the puppet expected to bring home the money.'

'Jesus, Tyler, someone had to help you. It's not like you were making waves on your own. A year unemployed. If I didn't push you, it would have never happened. I can't believe how ungrateful you are. I made sure we survived and didn't look like idiot paupers to our friends.'

He could feel the anger starting to swell. Once she was able to bring out a sense of love and need to protect her. Now he associated her with rage and stubbornness. 'Let's get this right.

They were your friends you were trying to keep up appearances for. Not mine. Mine were all made to feel unwelcome. You made me push them out.'

'Your friends were pigs. Common and beneath us.'

'Bullshit. They were my friends and would do anything for me. If there is one thing I regret, it's letting you push them out without stopping you. Anyway, it's nothing to do with you anymore. It's done. I've made my decision.'

She glared at him, balling her hands into fists at her side. 'And that's it. You're just going to leave? Quit your job, sell the house, and go. What about the furniture? What about the possessions?'

'I'm selling everything. I want a clean break.' He was going to add again how everything in the house was associated with her and he didn't want any reminders but decided it would be cruel to keep hammering home the point, and despite his dislike of the woman he once thought he was going to spend the rest of his life with, he didn't want to make it any harder on either of them than it had to be. It was true, though. Her fingerprints were all over that house. She had picked the furniture and decided the layout of each room. What they could have, what they couldn't, and he had gone along with it.

'You do know you're not a twenty-year-old kid anymore? What are you going to do with yourself one you are free from the shackles of responsibility?'

'You talk like I'm old,' he snapped, hurt by her tone.

'You'll be forty in a couple of years. Too old to sell everything you own and go travelling the world on a whim. Where the hell do you plan on going? How will you support yourself?'

'The money from the house sale will keep me going. I suppose that's one thing I'm fortunate about, that I kept that in my name without transferring half to you.'

She flinched again, and for a split second, he felt remorse, then ashamed that he was letting things get nasty. He took a deep breath and tried to regain his composure.

'I'm not sure where I'll go yet. Maybe Thailand to start then go from there. Wherever my head takes me. It will be nice to be free of the rat race for a while.'

She exhaled, shoulders slumping. He knew this routine. She was about to try and reason with him and make him feel guilty, a tactic used to great effect in the past.

'Look,' she said, taking a half step towards the open door. He could smell her perfume and in the back of his mind wondered if he had bought her it or if Tim had. 'I get that you feel like this is the right thing to do, but think about what you will be throwing away. You're literally selling your life. What will you be left with?'

'I don't need anything. Not from here. Too many bad memories around here, Amy. You. Tim, this house. All blame aside I need a clean break.'

'Then have one. Stay in the city, I'll give you the space you need, we can talk in a few weeks, I'll talk to Robert and see if he can get your job back i—'

'You're doing it again.'

'Doing what?' she snapped.

'Trying to run my life for me. I'm not a kid, Amy. I don't need someone to tell me when to go to sleep, what to eat, what to wear. Jesus, why can't you accept that this is over? I don't want to try again. I don't want to fix our marriage. I want to be by myself. Maybe one day we can be friends, but that's all it will ever be.'

'You would really throw all this away?' She was giving him that look, trying to be seductive. He saw through it, though and wondered how it had ever swayed him in the past.

He almost laughed but managed to keep a straight face at the way she had said *all this* as if his life had been anything other than as an extension of her. 'I don't know how many more times I have to tell you. It's done. We're finished. Nothing you can say or do will change my mind.'

'No, it can't be. I made a mistake with Tim, I get that, and I regret it every day. I'll never forgive myself. That's all over now, I want to come back to you, I want us to fix this situation.'

If it were a movie or a book, Tyler would have glared at her and said something dramatic. Maybe something like 'I'll never forgive you either,' or something equally damaging that would make him feel good. Instead, he decided to avoid any further confrontation and settled for the least inflammatory response he could.

'Yeah.'

'Well, I refuse to believe it's over. I'll fight as long as I have to I'll do it until you see sense i—' She froze, staring at the brown envelope he was holding towards her. 'What's that?'

He didn't answer. She knew what they were. She had to know they had been coming.

'Divorce papers?' she said, for the first time realising he was serious.

Bingo, baby, his cool inner self said. The actual Tyler made fists with his toes in the carpet ala John MacLaine and waited for her to take the envelope.

She shook her head and stepped back, taking the scent of her perfume with her. 'No. I won't take those.'

'That's up to you. My lawyer can always mail them to you. It just needs your signature.'

'I won't let you do this, I won't throw our marriage away,' she said, but she took the envelope, clutching it to her chest.

'The sooner you accept it's over, the sooner we can both move on.' *Maybe Tim will have you back*. He wanted to add that at the end and congratulated himself for holding back. He was about to close the door when she lurched towards him and grabbed his face, kissing him hard, probing her tongue into his mouth.

'Let me make it up to you. Let me show you how much I love you,' she panted, reaching for the clasp on his belt.

Uh-oh. This was bad. He was mentally strong and determined to do what he wanted, but the fact remained that his soon to be ex-wife was still incredibly attractive. Long red hair and green eyes, pale skin with a dash of freckles across her nose. Up close, he could smell her sweet scent of perfume and soap. She smelled clean, she smelled amazing. He was strong, but he wasn't Superman. Like most men, it wasn't always his brain that did the thinking. He started to kiss her back, pulling her towards him and thinking about what was to follow. A spectacular time in the bedroom no doubt, then... Then it would be back to how it was before. Back to a life he hated; he was nothing but a puppet to her.

He pushed her away, holding her at arm's length. 'No, I won't do this. It's not right.'

She glanced at the front of his jeans, still trying to use her body to win him over. 'That says otherwise,' she whispered, half-smiling.

'No, I'm sorry. I've made my decision. I don't need you. I don't deserve this.'

He saw her hope fade and melt back into the impostor he had grown to know. It was remarkable. The sneer, the hardness around the edges came back and he realised that as beautiful as she was externally, inside she was still black and rotten. 'It's over, Amy.'

'What makes you think you can last out there by yourself?' she hissed at him, tears streaming, lip trembling. She wasn't used to not getting her own way and he wasn't sure if it was genuine or part of the act but didn't care either way. 'You alone in the world. It' not a safe place, Tyler. There are crimes, murders. Fucking terrorists. You can live a safe life here. We can build something together. I'll change if that's what it takes.'

He shook his head. He had heard all this before. Things always seemed better for a week or so, then reverted to their old ways. 'No. I need to be alone. I have issues I need to work out.'

'Issues? You mean the drinking? Well, I've told you before, Tyler. You can't run away from it. No matter where you go, you'll still find yourself lost in the bottom of a bottle or propping up a bar somewhere.'

'Maybe so, but that's my decision to make. I'll fix things my way, without your help.'

'And how many years have you been saying that? Two? Three? You can't stop. That's what drove us apart. You can't leave the drink alone.'

He didn't want to get into that topic again, mostly because he knew she had a point. He was a borderline alcoholic, and maybe borderline was leaning on the optimistic side. He drank every day, most of the time heavily, and it was starting to take its toll. As if reading his thoughts, she went on. 'I mean look at you, Jesus, have a shave, clean yourself up. You've got fat. Look at that stomach.'

He knew she was saying it to hurt him. This was her way when things didn't go to plan, but he couldn't deny that either.

He looked at his T-shirt and the paunch that strained against the material. 'Look, are you going to sign the papers or not? I'm leaving in a couple of weeks and I want this all sorted out by then.'

'I don't want to sign the fucking papers.' She rarely shouted, swore even less and he knew he had struck a chord. He waited as she took a breath and composed herself. 'How am I supposed to find you if I have questions? You should at least stay until this is resolved.'

'My lawyer is dealing with it. My side of the papers is already signed. It's just waiting for you to do your part.'

She looked at the envelope, then at Tyler. 'You're not changing your mind, are you?'

He shook his head, and she seemed to deflate. 'That surprises you, doesn't it?'

She nodded. 'This isn't like you, Tyler. You were never so...'

'Adventurous.'

'I was going to say impulsive, but it serves the same purpose. Why can't you see that this is a huge mistake? I know you, this isn't you.'

'I know me, too, and I know it is me. This is what I want. This is what has to happen. Like it or not, we've both changed over the years. Even without the whole Tim situation, I think this would have been inevitable eventually.'

She sighed, giving up the fight and giving him the rarest of things: A victory. 'So what now?' she asked.

'Sign the papers once you've had them looked over and send them back to my lawyer. His contact info is in the envelope with the documents.'

'Please tell me you've at least kept the savings account, something to fall back on.'

He shook his head. 'I'm all in on this. I've lived safe for too long. I don't want something to fall back on. All I want to do is enjoy life for a while. Everything else is just stuff.'

She had grown cold again, and that sneer was reappearing as she spoke. 'At least tell the truth, Tyler. We both know you will piss all the money away on booze and will be back here within a few weeks with nothing to show for it. You might hate me and I get it, but I'm trying to help you. You need someone in your life to tell you what to do. You can't do it by yourself.'

He looked at her, searching to see if the woman he once loved was there, even a small part of her. If he could find it, then he might consider staying. He knew though, as he looked into her eyes, that anything they once had was dead. Whatever was once there had fizzled away to the point that they may as well have been strangers.

'I'm done talking about this, Amy. Sign the papers or don't. Either way, I'm leaving in a couple of weeks. I'd hoped we could do this in a civil way with minimal fuss. I can't do any more than that.'

'You're going to end up drinking yourself to death in some foreign country and nobody will know about it. You need me in your life, Tyler. You can't function without me.'

'Sign the papers,' he said, gently ushering her out of the door. They looked at each other, those few seconds seeming to last a lifetime and say more than words ever could, then Tyler closed the door and felt as if a huge weight had been lifted from his shoulders.

CHAPTER TWO

NEPTUNE'S FOLLY - five miles off the coast of Devil's Island, Australia.

'You've heard of the shark, right?'

Scott looked at his friend, smiled and then took a drink of his beer. 'What shark?'

'Come on, man, you must have heard of it,' Karl said, taking a drag on the joint and handing it over.

Scott inhaled, blowing smoke into the warm air. The sun was low, an orange ball balanced on the horizon throwing out an undulating golden carpet on the water. 'I have no idea what you're talking about.'

Karl grinned and shifted position. 'This area we're in now is like Australia's answer to the Bermuda Triangle.'

'Yeah, right,' Scott said.

'No, it's true. People have known about it for years but nobody says anything because they don't want idiots swarming over here and killing the tourist trade.'

Scott looked at his friend, assessed his skinny features, and saw there was no sign of a lie in his words. 'Alright, I'll humour you. Tell me about it.'

Karl took a sip of his beer and ran a hand through his blond hair. 'Word is that there's this area where boats go missing but nobody really knows why. Legend says there is a monster shark down there that attacks and sinks any boat that ventures into its territory.'

'And yet here we are. Unharmed and alive,' Scott fired back, disappointed that his friend couldn't at least be creative. Sensing that Scott was losing interest, Karl went on.

'It's not just that. There's more.'

'There always is,' Scott sighed.

'No, listen. A couple of years ago, rumour has it that a drug runner was on its way to make a delivery of gold bars that had been stolen from this cartel. It was supposed to drop off in one of the little island coves here on the coast but it never arrived at the destination. Most people say the cartel found their stash and intercepted it before it could be delivered. The other story is that it strayed into the shark's territory and it sank his boat, gold and all.'

'That's the stupidest thing I've ever heard. Someone would have been down there and brought it up, shark or not.'

'They did,' Karl said. 'A guy who my brother knows said he dived down there and there was gold all over the sea floor. Bars of it just waiting to be found.'

'And still, nobody has bothered to go get it?'

Karl shook his head. 'People are too scared. People go down there and never come back up.'

'And this friend of yours.'

'My brother's friend.'

'Yeah him. Did he come up with gold? Is he rich now?'

'Nah, he said he got spooked. Feels like you're being watched down there so he came back to the surface.'

'Convenient,' Scott said.

'I'm telling you, there's money to be had if you have the guts.'

The combination of bravado and alcohol took over Scott's rationale, and he stood. 'Alright.'

'Alright, what?'

'I've got a tank and wet suit in the galley. I'll go take a look and see if this gold stash is down there.'

'Yeah, right,' Karl said, sipping his drink. Scott went below and started rummaging around in the galley. 'Wait, you're serious?'

Scott returned with the oxygen tank and goggles and a pair of flippers under his arm. 'Why not? If there's gold down there just waiting to be claimed, I'm up for it. Everyone wants to be rich, right?'

'Yeah but…Come on, this is stupid. I was just messing with you, man.' Karl waited for Scott to laugh it off and open another beer, then realised he had no intention of doing either. Instead, he was checking the regulator of his air tanks and slipping his feet into the diving fins. 'You're actually going down there?'

'Why not? I've been diving for years. I'll disprove this legend one way or the other or I'll get rich trying. You coming?'

Karl shook his head. 'No. I'm too drunk and so are you. Besides, it will be full dark soon.'

Scott grinned and showed Karl the underwater torch. 'Any other objections?'

Karl shrugged. 'Suppose not.' He didn't believe the legends either, not really. Part of what he had said had been with the intention of getting a rise out of his friend. He never imagined he would go through with it and actually dive down there, which itself made him nervous. There was the whole 'what if' scenario. What if it were true? What if the legend was based on reality? Also, what if the gold was down there? He wasn't rich by any means and maybe if they did find gold, he could get a little bit of money, maybe a few girls and local fame to go with it all by sitting on the boat and waiting for his friend to go and have a look. It was a win-win situation for him.

Scott finished getting ready, taking a test breath on his regulator and putting the goggles over his head.

'What the hell am I supposed to do when you're down there?'

Scott moved to the transom and sat on it, grinning at his friend as he secured the tank on his back. 'Just wait here for me. Oh, and keep an eye out for sharks.'

'Yeah, right,' Karl muttered, glancing at the ever dipping sun. 'Hey, don't forget this.'

Karl crossed the deck and grabbed the torch and handed it to Scott.

'Thanks,' he said as he attached it to his diving belt. 'Who knows? Maybe this time tomorrow we'll be millionaires.'

Karl could see it now in the dusk light. Shadow of uncertainty in his friend's face.

'Look, Scott, forget this idea. Let's head back in, maybe go out for a few beers.'

'Sounds good. After I've checked.'

Karl opened his mouth to say more but knew there was little point. Scott put his eye mask on, put his regulator into his mouth then gave the thumbs up. Karl watched as he fell backwards over the side and disappeared into the black depths of the ocean.

***

It was like an alien world. No matter how many times he dived, Scott always felt a sense of wonder and amazement at being alone in the ocean. Even with dark approaching, the clear waters allowed him to see better than he could have hoped. Fish darted in front of his torch beam, every conceivable species and colour. He angled towards the bottom, enjoying his surroundings. A glorious coral reef undulated with the currents. As he swept his torch beam, he was treated to more spectacular sights as he made his way deeper, the only sound to break the silence the rhythm of his breath and the bubbles ejected from the regulator. A turtle swam across his field of vision and disappeared out of sight as he passed deeper than the natural light allowed, meaning only what was in the beam of his torch was visible to him. He didn't know how deep the waters were here and remembered to stay within his limitations. He wasn't too drunk yet but still knew that without the lowering of his inhibitions, he likely wouldn't have attempted such a dive. Something caught his eye, something huge and slate-coloured below him, a tapered body in his torch beam. It was only as the torch beam settled on the object did Scott realise that it wasn't the giant shark Karl had told him about, but the overturned hull of a boat. Scott kicked towards it, enjoying the burn in his lungs as the sandy ocean floor revealed itself to him. The boat he had seen was a fishing trawler. It lay on its side, its surface covered in rust and coral as the ocean reclaimed it. He stopped swimming, kicking in place and shining the torch beam all around him and wishing he had dived during the day when visibility would have been better. He could spot at least three other wrecks in his immediate vicinity, which at least made some part of the story true in that for whatever reason, ships sank in that particular area of the ocean. On the seabed, there was, as expected a wide debris field from the wrecks. With the idea that the stories about gold a little bit less far-fetched, he skimmed his torch across the ground and started to explore the debris. Most of it was garbage. Petrified wood or broken pieces of hull. He saw rusty cutlery, old cans and plates. A long-abandoned crab pot thick with rust. An uneasy feeling came over him as he scoured the debris, but he wasn't sure if there was a reason for it or if it was just the story his friend had told him. He forced himself to remain calm and focus on his job. He poked around some more in the debris. He found a plastic chair. A broken television. A cracked toilet seat. No treasure. Nothing he would consider valuable. He realised then what it was that making him so paranoid. There were no other fish around. Often where there were wrecks, there were fish. The broken hulls of the boats made perfect environments for them, and yet there was nothing but him. He was sure something was moving, out on the edge of his peripheral vision. Scott stared into the dark, realising just how vulnerable he was then dismissing the idea. The story Karl had told him was making him jumpy for no reason at all. He turned his attention back to the seabed and poked around the debris a little more, and was about to give up when something caught his eye in the shadow of the overturned fishing trawler's hull. He swam to it, unable to help glancing behind him before returning his attention to the object he had seen. It was partially buried in the Sand. He set his torch on the sand and started to dig with both hands to free the object, unable to believe what he was seeing. The gold bar was around ten inches long and much heavier than he anticipated. He held it, rotating the bar in the light of the torch beam. If there was one, there would be more. That he was sure of. There was no way he could carry the bar back to the surface, as it was far too heavy. He set it on the sand and considered his options, the excitement hindering rational thought. Something happened then. A change in the current, a rush of water pressing against him as if something big had moved close by. Scott spun around, back to the overturned hull, and stared out into the dark. Nothing moved, and yet that made it worse. The black depths betrayed no secrets, and the silence reminded him again how isolated he was. One thing he did know was that he didn't want to stay there any longer. The gold was going nowhere. He would resurface and think about what to do then come back later when it was lighter. He didn't like to admit he was afraid, but the stories Karl had told him were at the forefront of his mind and he badly wanted to be back on the surface. He started to ascend, forcing himself not to rush but also unable to shake the feeling he was being observed. He realised he had left his torch and could see its dull light illuminating the side of the overturned hull, then it was gone. He stopped swimming, confused that the light had gone out. Then it was back just as it was. He tried to convince himself that it had simply failed and lost power for a second and that what he thought he had seen was simply impossible. It looked, at a glance, that something had passed in front of the torch. Something so large that it had completely blocked out the light. That, he knew, was impossible. There was nothing big enough to do that, nothing he knew of that lived in those waters. He turned his attention back to reaching the surface, no longer enjoying the alien underwater world as he had just minutes earlier. It occurred to him that he was the alien. He was the stranger and didn't belong. Each passing moment, he wondered if something was going to come at him, a shape from the darkness, a hellish ring of jagged teeth. But he surfaced without harm, startling Karl who was sitting on the transom waiting for him.

'Jesus, you scared the hell out of me,' Karl said as he helped Scott onto the boat.

Still shaken, Scott took off his regulator and goggles, catching his breath and grateful to be back on the boat.

'Hey, you okay, man? You don't look too good.'

Scott nodded. 'I'm fine. It was cold down there.'

'You find anything?' Karl asked.

Without missing a beat, Scott shook his head. 'Not a thing. Whatever legend you've heard is bullshit. Nothing there but rocks and sand.'

Karl looked disappointed and grabbed another beer from the cool box. 'There goes the get rich quick idea.'

'Yeah,' Scott said as he dried his hair with a towel. 'Shit

happens, right?'

'Yeah.'

'Anyway, it's getting cold. Let's go in,' Scott said, moving into the warmth of the cabin and starting the engines. Before they set off, he made a note of the coordinates on his GPS for later when he intended to come back and make himself a very rich man. He steered the boat towards the scattering of lights on the mainland, leaving the gold and boat graveyard behind.

CHAPTER THREE

Nash knew that when even getting out of bed hurt, Father Time was really starting to put the boot in. He rolled to a sitting position, grunting and squinting against the sun which was obtrusive in its probing between the curtains. Once upon a time, the forty-five year old only felt this bad in the aftermath of one of his amateur boxing bouts, but now it took nothing but a night sleeping in the same position to fill him with aches and pains. He flexed his hands, muscles in his tanned forearms rippling beneath the fluff of hair which was now as white as that on his head. He grunted at the sun again, and rubbed his stubble-covered cheeks, knowing the day ahead wasn't going to be good. Usually, if he woke up with pain, it would stay with him until he tried to sleep again later. He found he could medicate it with drink, but didn't want to get into such a mug's game as that. Addiction was something he'd seen too much of back in his Army days. Addiction to alcohol or drugs was the breaking of many a good man, and so he avoided both.

He walked towards the bathroom, stifling a yawn and wondering if there was any way he could get out of going on the boat. Fishing used to be something he enjoyed until it was how he was forced to make a living. Now he hated it, the smell, the monotony, the uncertainty about if they would catch anything and be able to survive another day. Plus, there was the other thing to worry about. His plague, his nightmare. The curse he couldn't shake. He paused on his way to the bathroom as he did most mornings and looked at the folder on his dresser. He opened it, leafing through the papers inside. Reports. Sightings. Speculation. All about something that most people laughed off. Something he knew for a fact was true and that he had seen up close. His hand started to tremble, and a tear fell from his one remaining functional tear duct. He had tried to warn people about what he had seen, but when he told them what had happened to him, they laughed him off like he was some kind of crazy man. He could understand that. Even to him, the story seemed like it couldn't be true. He had asked himself if he had exaggerated what he had seen, if the terror and fear of death had skewed things in his mind, but he didn't think so. What he had experienced was as fresh now almost thirty years after the fact and was exactly as he remembered it. He closed the folder and continued on to the bathroom. It was still dim, the sun not yet reaching that side of the house. He pulled the string for the light, waiting until it flickered into life and bathed the room in its sterile artificial glow. The abomination in the mirror had long ago stopped frightening him. Now it just terrified others and made any hope of a social life next to impossible. He stood and started to brush the teeth he had left on the right side of his mouth. The left side had been pulverised during the attack to the point where he should have died. This, he mused, should have been his evidence. If they had measured the wounds, they would have been able to tell how big the teeth were of the thing that had done this to him. Instead, they told him he was imagining things and that it was just a large shark that had attacked and decided for whatever reason to let him live. They told him he was lucky and he should be grateful. He spat in the sink and rinsed his mouth, then put his half denture in, filling the hollow, sunken look that filled half his face. The eye on that side was sightless, a milky orb which still saw the horrors that had happened to him that day. No hair grew on the right side of his head. His natural scalp had been removed during the attack. The skin that replaced it was grafted from the rest of his body, leaving a bumpy alien landscape filled with ruts and scars. His lower lip had been lost, and the resulting graft made him look as if he was melting. Granted, the doctors had done a remarkable job to put him back together, but sometimes, when he was at his loneliest and trying to figure out what the point of his existence was, he sometimes wished he had died instead of being saved. It would have been better than such a lonely existence where it was just him and his scrapbook, a collection of sightings and speculation which only made him question if things had been as he recalled them or if, as the authorities suggested, his frightened mind had simply exaggerated it and made it into something impossible. He didn't think so. As broken down as his body may be, his mind was still sharp when it came to that day. The smell of salt and blood in the water. The fire licking at the overturned hull and spewing black smoke against the pale blue sky as the ocean prepared to take another victim. The fin, huge and scarred, a slate grey wedge of terror as it cut towards the stranded crew. Watching as it took them not one at a time from beneath, but in twos or threes at once. The pull of the water as it moved underneath him, the wake pushing him back twenty feet as it claimed more victims. Then the waiting. Waiting for his turn, waiting to be taken. And yes, being lucky. Because as devastating as the injuries to his face and shoulders were, as bad as the shattered bones had been, it was a glancing blow. It surfaced without warning. It's mouth a pink maw, a cavernous passage straight to hell. The two men in front of him may have screamed or it may have been him. The beast's jaw closed, the two men pulverised in a bloody froth of bone and flesh, but he suffered only a glancing blow, the serrated teeth closing in him and doing damage but not taking him down, not into the depths with the others. Bobbing there waiting to die, face hanging off and dripping into the warm waters, bones shattered in their shredded skin coverings. Smoke, salt, and blood burning his nostrils, his tongue lolling out of the gaping hole where his cheek once was. Then the waiting. Waiting to be taken waiting to be next. A dull explosion as the boat went under, water rushing to swallow it as its distressed hill creaked in protest. Then nothing. Silence. Darkness until he woke in the hospital, a rearranged, man-shaped jigsaw puzzle. Then, it was just snatches. Hazy memories. Someone giving him the last rights. A man saying how he had pulled him onto a lifeboat. A group of doctors by his bedside sure he wouldn't last the night.

Nash gripped the edge of the sink and looked away from his reflection, the face of a dead man who somehow survived against the odds. Unable to stand looking at it any longer, he went back into his bedroom and dressed.

#

Across town, just as Nash was battling his demons and preparing to face another day, Tyler Matthews was waking up, face buried in the carpet of a cheap motel. His mouth had the unmistakable aftertaste of another night of debauchery, and he could feel his head pulsing with the familiar rhythm of a hangover. He pushed himself into a sitting position and looked around the room. At least he had made it to the bedroom this time, if not the bed itself. He was still in last night's clothes, and only then realised the awful smell was him. He saw the empty Jack Daniels bottle by the bed and then the overstuffed ashtray and realised Amy had been right. No matter how far he went, his problems would just follow him. It had been two years since he walked out on his life. He had travelled across America, exploring the small towns and drifting wherever his instinct told him to go, invariably a place where he could get a drink. That, at least, hadn't changed. Although he tried to convince himself that he was on a journey of exploration and self-discovery, in reality, it was just a huge tour of the bars and dives of the world, each smoky, sweaty watering hole leading him to the next. New Orleans had been particularly eventful; the drinks were cool and the weather and women were hot. He thought that when it eventually came to settling down and getting some kind of life in order, that was the place he would like to go. Once he had finished his lazy jaunt across America, he had moved over to Europe, which he didn't like as much. After the joys of the Deep South, the hospitality and friendliness to strangers in Europe was lacking. Most treated him with a cold sense of indifference, especially when the drink took over and he became the foul-mouthed violent demon he kept locked away most of the time. Some parts of Europe were better. Spain and Italy were nice. Switzerland was beautiful and relaxed, Russia large and intimidating. Despite Amy's misgivings, he had taken to life on the road well and was thrilled to be out of the rat race. There was a simple sense of joy of knowing everything he owned was in his backpack and he didn't know where he would be resting his head until he arrived there. He had lost weight and grown a beard. Back in his old life, he used to dye his hair black to hide the onset of age. Now he had a shoulder-length, salt-and-pepper style. During his journey, he had met some wonderful people with amazing stories to tell. He had experienced tragedy and joy, seen violence and compassion. There were no regrets apart from wishing he had done it sooner. His body felt old, that much was true, no doubt in part to his constant alcohol abuse which had escalated now that he didn't have to fit it around a nine-to-five day job. When there was nothing else to do, it was never too early for a drink. He glanced at his watch, squinting to see the display. It was a little after ten in the morning which meant the bars would be open. Pushing himself up off the floor, he staggered to the window and looked out at another crisp Australian morning. Of everywhere he had been, he was starting to think Australia was a close contender with New Orleans for where he might like to settle when the time came. He liked the heat, and the people were as friendly as those in the Mid-South. People, though, were not what he needed right now. His body craved alcohol and he had learned that denying it was pointless. He considered showering but settled instead for throwing on a different T-shirt from the pile in the corner, spraying a little deodorant, and heading out to find somewhere to feed his craving.

CHAPTER FOUR

NEPTUNE'S FOLLY - five miles off the coast of Devil's Island, Australia.

Scott brought the boat to a halt then looked at his older brother. 'Alright, this is it.'

'You sure?' Paul said, standing at the stern and peering into the sun-dappled waters.

Scott double checked the coordinates. 'Yeah. This is it.'

'You better not be wasting my fucking time, Scotty.'

'You think I'd go this far on a prank?'

'No, I suppose not. Come on, let's suit up.'

Paul was Scott's sibling, and at thirty-one, was older than him by seven years. The last five of those years he had spent in jail for hiding a friend who had committed an armed robbery in his house. One of the bank tellers had been shot in the robbery, and although he made it to the hospital, died later. Paul didn't realise it was a murder his friend was wanted for until it was too late, and so got caught up in the fallout. He met some bad people when he was locked up and had come out a tougher, more cynical man than when he went in. It had also ruined his potential career in engineering. With a criminal record, work was impossible to come by which increased the bitterness he felt towards society. Where Scott was slender and athletic with well-defined muscles and an even tan, Paul was shorter and more muscular, his arms like concrete, his neck a tree trunk. For their physical differences, the two brothers had come together united by the one thing that was the curse of mankind and the cause of countless problems around the globe.

Money.

Scott had told him of the discovery he had made, about the legend and the gold. To his surprise, Paul knew of the legend. He said kids used to call it the Devil's Triangle when he was younger but had always assumed it was another urban legend like the Samsonite scarecrows, the supermarket run by vampires, or the story about the Slenderman. With no job and no prospects, it hadn't taken Scott much convincing to get his brother to go with him to the spot to take a look. Scott wanted to come back at night under cover of darkness, but Paul had refused, saying it would look suspicious if they were out there at night. It was better, he said, to go during the day so that if anyone did query them, they could say they were just enjoying the sun and doing a little snorkelling.

Scott moved to the stern, helping Paul unpack the bag he had brought on board.

'What are these for again?' he asked as he pulled the heavy plastic out of the bag.

'Flotation balloons. If there is gold down there, it's going to be too hard to carry.'

'There *is* gold down there and it *is* heavy,' Scott said as they lay the contents of the bag out on the rear deck.

'Relax, Scotty. I wasn't doubting you. I'm here, aren't I?

'Yeah, sorry, I just…this could change our lives, you know?'

'Yeah, it could,' Paul said, looking out over the gloriously crisp blue waters. 'Anyway, to finish answering your question, these flotation balloons will be how we get the haul to the surface. They're weighted and go down with us deflated like this. There's a net underneath that we put our haul into on the seabed. All we do then is activate the inflator here.' He pointed to a pulley on the side of the deflated red bag. 'The unit then auto-inflates and floats our haul to the surface. We follow it up all the way. Easy.'

Scott nodded. 'Alright, I can get on board with that.'

'Good. Then help me get everything ready so we can stop wasting daylight and get down there.'

II

Half an hour later, the two brothers were in the water. They had already sunk the flotation balloons, dropping them overboard and watching them sink into the ocean depths. They now followed, swimming in tandem. Scott had neglected to tell his brother about the uneasy feeling he'd had in the boat graveyard, and supposed that if he was aware of the legend, then he knew what was said to be down there. Fortunately for Scott, the entire scene felt a lot less intimidating in full daylight. The visibility was superb, the sun filtering through in undulating golden shafts, reminding Scott of the joys of this secret world beneath the waves. Schools of multi-coloured fish swam around them, moving to accommodate the much bigger lifeforms as they descended into the dark. It was only when they had descended beyond the reach of the sun's rays and had to activate their head-mounted underwater lamps did the joy Scott had felt transform back into the creeping sense of dread and the unshakable feeling that something was watching them from the periphery of their vision. There was something below them. Scott saw it and pointed. It looked like blood, like something had been attacked below. Scenarios raced through Scott's mind about the truth behind the legend and how they were about to become part of it forever. He could imagine years from now people sitting around a camp fire discussing urban legends and asking if anyone had heard the story of the two treasure-hunting brothers who had met their end diving for gold in Devil's Triangle and were never to be seen again. It was only as he fully allowed his light to shine on it that he realized it wasn't blood, but the flotation balloon they had sunk. It was half-folded over in the debris field, the waterproof material swaying in the currents, the air canisters on their side on the seabed. He gestured to Scott and pointed, and the two dived for the balloon. As they neared the seabed, the graveyard of ships bones became visible. Barnacle-encrusted relics scattered across a much wider area than Scott had first thought during his last dive. He immediately recognized the overturned fishing vessel on its side. They had come in at a slightly different angle to the one he had on his last dive, and he was able to see the upper structure of the boat half-buried in the sand. He was amazed to see that despite the damaged caused during its sinking, some of the wheelhouse windows were unbroken, reflecting his torch beam as he passed it over the hull. He motioned for Paul to follow, heading back to the area where he had found the gold bar. As before, there were no fish that he could see. They were in a void, a wide open expanse of water in which they appeared to be the only living creatures. Pushing it aside and thinking of the end goal, he approached the hull, relieved to see his torch where he had left it, its battery dead. He also saw the gold bar beside it. He increased his speed, excited to show his brother that his find was real. He picked up the bar and turned to face Paul, who was lagging behind and dragging the flotation balloon behind him. Elated, Scott held up the bar. Paul swam over and took it from him, turning the heavy bar over in his hands. They eyes met, the thrill and excitement of what would be a life-changing experience shared between them. Paul put the bar in the net under the flotation balloons then started to sift through the debris on the ocean floor. Following the lead of his brother, Scott did the same. Moving aside broken wood and scrabbling through the loose sand in an effort to uncover whatever treasures lurked beneath. He moved a splintered sheet of carbon fibre hull aside and was about to search beneath it when he flicked his head towards the darkness of the ocean beyond. He had sensed something moving. More than that, he had felt it. A current tugging against him as something big moved close by. He let the sheet of carbon fibre fall back to the ocean floor and stared out into the void, once again filled with that same sense of being watched or worse — stalked. He looked to his brother, wishing he could shout to him or suggest they leave, but Paul was focused on searching for more gold, tossing aside wreckage in his efforts to better his life. Scott was watching him, wondering how to communicate that he wanted to surface when he saw it. At first, he thought it was a submarine coming towards them, then he saw the curvature of the snout as the creature came from the dark heading straight for Paul. He had seen sharks before, of course. They had seen them in the aquarium where they swam around the sunken Perspex tunnels. Nothing comparable to the behemoth that came towards them. Scott tried to put it into context, to compare it to something he had seen in the real world to give some kind of rationality to how big it was and could think of nothing. It was almost leisurely as it came out of the darkness, a flick of the tail moving it within ten feet of Paul who was so preoccupied with his search he hadn't seen it. Its skin was the color of slate and pocked with scars, old and new. Black emotionless dolls eyes the size of a basketball watched its prey, mouth partially open to allow the water to flow through, the tips of its twelve inch serrated teeth visible. An old harpoon was embedded in its side, trailing a frayed trail of rope behind it, the skin around the wound healed and making the harpoon part of the giant shark's anatomy. It was at this point, as Scott looked on unable to move, that Paul saw it. He lurched back as the shark approached, kicking up loose sand from the sea floor. Scott was sure the shark was going to attack, but instead it circled Paul, dump truck-sized head swaying back and forth as it assessed this new creature which had encroached on its territory. As it moved around his brother, Scott could see the full scale of the behemoth. Paul watched, knowing he was powerless to do anything but wait and see what would happen next. The creature moved closer and Scott was sure they were about to die, but the shark seemed uncertain, and backed away, continuing to circle Paul. Scott knew he had to do something to distract the shark and help his brother. His eyes went to the flotation balloon which was ten feet away from him and a further twenty feet away from the huge shark circling his brother. Although every instinct screamed at him and told him he was crazy, he moved towards the balloon, keeping low and close to the seabed. Still the shark circled, trying to decide if such small prey was worth bothering with. Scott reached the flotation balloon, looking at the cylinders of gas. The device was simple enough to use. There was a chord attached to the tanks which would break the interior seal and fill the balloons with air and send it on its slow ascent to the surface. He hoped it would distract the shark into giving chase so he and his brother could escape. For Scott, the gold could stay in the graveyard of boats. He didn't care anymore. Now all he wanted was to survive. Hands trembling, he waited for the shark to circle away from him then pulled the chord. The balloons inflated a pneumatic hiss as the air was released into them sending a torrent of bubbles towards the surface. Scott swam to the hull of the nearest overturned vessel, pressing himself against it as the balloons started to ascend. The shark changed course to investigate, circling the balloons as they rose. Scott watched it go, unable to take in the size of it. He turned his attention to Paul, hoping to signal for him that they should leave, but Paul was already swimming, angling up and away from the shark back towards the boat. For a while, Scott didn't think he would be able to follow. He was so terrified that he couldn't move. It was only the idea of the shark coming back and crushing him in its massive jaws that made him move. He followed his brother, closing the distance between them. On the surface, his brother's bulk helped him. Underwater, Scott's smaller, more athletic frame was better for moving through the water. He closed the distance, looking for the shark but unable to see it. The two siblings swam in tandem, the water growing lighter as they neared the surface and the dark shadow of the boat, desperate for the safety it would provide. Paul was starting to slow, and Scott moved ahead. He checked behind him and saw Paul still coming, his eyes wide and filled with something Scott had never seen before.

Fear.

Scott couldn't see the shark and thought they might just make it. He broke the surface, the hull of the boat appearing as an impassable white tower of carbon fibre. He swam to the steel rungs of the ladder and started to pull himself out just as Scott broke the surface and tore his regulator out of his mouth.

'Hurry up, Scotty, climb quicker. Get the hell out,' he shrieked. Distracted, Scott slipped on the rung and fell back into the water. He started to climb again but Paul was too terrified to be rational. He pulled his brother aside and started to climb up himself, scrabbling to get out of the water. Scott dipped his head beneath the waves, unable to resist looking and wishing he hadn't. That bus-sized head was beneath them, ascending at speed, mouth open to reveal the abyss beyond and the death it would bring. He knew he could never climb out in time. He was tired, the terror compelling him to kick in place and watch it come for him. He wondered how it would feel when those jaws closed around him. He wondered if he would feel his bones splinter or his guts eject themselves from his body as he was devoured. Something grabbed him, but it wasn't the shark. Strong hands from the surface pulling him clear out of the water. His brother, his blessed brother, who after spending all of his jail time bulking up in the gym, could easily lift a hundred and seventy pounds of dead weight sibling out of the water. Paul grunted as he lifted Scott free of the water, both of them collapsing onto the deck. Scott spat out his regulator, wanting to say so much. He was angry, scared, elated, and grateful. He turned to his brother, unsure if he wanted to thank him or hit him for pulling him off the ladder when the forty foot vessel exploded from beneath as the seventy-seven-foot shark smashed into the bottom of the hull, shattering the boat and throwing both Scott and Paul back into the water. Scott breathed in, taking sea water into his lungs. He coughed and spluttered, trying not to panic. The boat looked as if it had been hit by a missile and was already sinking beneath the waves, a fine carpet of debris bobbing on the surface. Scott knew it was bad. They were miles from land, and apart from the small scattering of uninhabited islands, there was nobody close who could help. He looked around for Paul but couldn't see him. He saw the fin break the surface out of his peripheral vision. He turned to face it, watching as it came towards him, a six-foot-tall triangle of death as it cut through the water. In the movies, people always escaped situations like this. But he knew it was over. There was no help. No way to escape the grim reaper as it breathed its cold breath on his neck. The shark broke the surface, mouth opening ready to take him, its teeth covered in chunks of bloody meat.

'So that's where Paul went.'

It was the last thought he had before his body was pulverised, taken in one bite by the mammoth creature which knew only its instinct to feed. Silence fell over the debris field, the splintered boat remains bobbing on the surface. Ten feet away, the red flotation balloon broke the surface and waited to be retrieved.

CHAPTER FIVE

Tyler had learned during the course of his travels to avoid the tourist spots. Although he was technically in that category himself, he had found that not only were the spots the locals drank in cheaper, they were also less rowdy and without the drunk holidaymakers who didn't care about those who had serious drinking to do. He was certain that the current watering hole he was in, aptly named Roaches, wouldn't be troubled by tourists. It was dark, the shadows heavy against the baking Australian heat which was kept at bay by the air conditioning. This was a spot for the people who lived in the area. The ones who worked nights and might have come in for a quick post-work drink before slipping away to get some sleep, or those who were without work and had nothing to do. It was also a place for people like him — professional drinkers with a habit to feed — something which he had learned people in every country he had visited had learned to spot. He wondered if he really looked that shitty and his ex-wife's words echoed in his brain. He was aware of the consequences of heavy drinking. His father had died from alcoholism as had his father before him. Tyler supposed it was a family trait, something he had inherited along with the hooked nose and dry sense of humour. It wasn't even that he was depressed and was trying to drink himself to death, he was just weak when it came to addiction and didn't have the ability to say no.

He sat at the end of the bar, reading the previous day's newspaper and working on his third beer with a Jack Daniels chaser and wondering if it was time to move on to a new area. Funds were starting to deplete, the money he had got for the house, his car and his possessions starting to dwindle. The idea of going back to society seemed alien to him, especially after seeing all that life had to offer outside of the grind. He wondered how it would be, to go back to his old life. To see Amy again. He supposed it would be awkward. She would be angry and remind him she was right about his inability to kick the booze.

Fuck her.

He swallowed his JD in one, closing his eyes as its warmth radiated through his body.

Screw you, Amy.

He stopped himself before his thoughts turned nasty. When that happened, the alcohol demon he carried around inside him would wake and get out of control. When that happened, he would black out and have no idea what happened next. Those incidents scared him. He would often wake up asleep in the street or in a jail cell. He knew it was only a matter of time before he did something he couldn't shy away from when nursing a hangover. Even though he tried not to think about her, Amy was right. He needed to keep control of his habit and make sure he kept it in check. Even as the thought crossed his mind, he ordered another drink, nodding to the bartender to bring him another and making the whole notion he had any control over his addiction irrelevant. As he waited for his drink to arrive, he looked around the bar at the few drinkers scattered around the room who Tyler assumed were pro drinkers like him. Around the curve of the bar just a few feet away, two men were deep in conversation. One of them was horrifically scarred, and even with the Panama hat pulled low on his head, Tyler could see something severe had happened to him. The man next to him was in his twenties, skin tanned, black hair and blue eyes, the kind of guy women always threw themselves at. The scarred man was clearly frustrated, his hands gesticulating as he spoke to the younger man. Tyler had no intent to listen in on their conversation, it just happened as he waited for his drink. The old man kept mentioning gold, and how they could be rich to which the younger man was telling him it was likely a hoax and he shouldn't get his hopes up. The younger of the two men caught Tyler watching them.

'Can I help you?' he snapped.

Tyler stammered, stumbling over his words. 'No, sorry, I wasn't trying to be nosy, I was just waiting for my drink and couldn't help but overhear.'

'See, Dad?' the younger man said. 'Everyone can hear you making a fool out of yourself.'

The scarred man looked at his son, then across at Tyler. 'You're a regular in here, aren't you?'

Tyler nodded.

'Thought so. I've seen you in here before.'

Tyler didn't reply. He had never seen the scarred man before. He would have recognised him. The man with the scars grinned as if reading his thoughts. 'Don't worry, I'm not surprised you haven't seen me. I usually sit in the corner where it's dark and my son here, Liam, gets me my drinks. I don't want to scare off the customers.' He tried to smile, but with his lack of lips and facial muscle structure, it came off as a grimace. The man held his good hand out to Tyler. 'Names Nash. Robert Nash.'

The two men shook hands. 'Tyler. Nice to meet you.'

Nash flicked his head towards his son. 'This short-tempered one is my son, Liam.'

Liam nodded at Tyler, showing none of the warmth or friendliness of his father

'I'm impressed,' Nash said.

'Excuse me?' Tyler said as the bartender set his drinks in front of him and took the empties away along with the money.

'You look me in the eye when you talk to me. Most people see this and think I'm some sort of leper.'

'I take people as I find them.'

'That accent. You're not a local, are you? You a yank?'

'Yeah.'

'Most of the tourists stick to the coastal bars, but something tells me that's not you either.'

'No, I'm…well, to tell you the truth, I don't know what I am. I sold everything I own and decided I wanted to travel. Been doing that for a while now and found myself here. I don't like the tourist places.'

'I don't blame you, mate. Too pricey and rowdy. This is a decent spot, though, even though the draft stuff is watered-down piss.'

Tyler grinned. He liked Nash already. Living with such a disfigurement couldn't have been easy, yet he seemed to be in good spirits.

'We don't have time for this, Dad,' Liam said, giving a mistrustful glance towards Tyler.

'Of course we do. This isn't time limited, son. Now go get the drinks in whilst I bring our new friend up to speed and see what his opinion is on this.'

'Dad…'

'Another beer for me and whatever you want.' Nash cut in.

Liam glared at his father, then at Nash before doing as he was told and heading to the bar. Nash watched him go, then turned back to Tyler. 'He's a good kid, just stubborn. I can't say too much as he gets it from me.'

Tyler nodded and sipped his drink.

'How much did you hear about what me and the boy were

saying?'

Tyler shrugged. 'Nothing really. Something about gold but no details.'

'Right, right, well, the thing is, me and him are in a bit of disagreement about something and I thought that you, as a neutral, might be able to help us out.'

'Sure, why not?' Tyler said, amazed at how quickly he had got used to Nash's horrific scars.

'Let me ask you something, mate,' Nash said. 'You ever hear of the Devil's Triangle?'

Tyler shook his head. 'Should I have?'

'Probably not. It's more of a local legend.'

'What is it?'

Nash looked around and tried to grin again, the effect ghastly. 'Well, it's this place about a hundred miles off the coast. An area where people don't go.'

'Why's that?' Tyler asked, thinking this was starting to sound like the start of a corny ghost story.

'You heard of the Bermuda Triangle? Surely you know that one.'

'Yeah, ship graveyard. They say weird things happen there. Magnetic interference or something. Causes boats to lose their way and planes to crash.'

'Yeah, that's the one,' Nash said as Liam returned with the drinks. 'Well, we got one of those here only we call it the Devil's Triangle.'

'I've never heard of it.'

'You won't have,' Liam said. 'People down here don't talk about it. They don't even take it seriously, which is what I'm trying to tell the old man here.'

Nash raised a gnarled, scar-crossed hand. 'Hang on a second, you're getting ahead of the story, son.'

Tyler waited until Nash took a sip of his drink then went on. 'Anyway, this place, the Devil's Triangle, people have talked for years about it. It was first reported back in 1877 as a place to avoid because it was dangerous there. Ship graveyard.'

'Could be shallow waters. It happens.'

Liam grinned. 'You think nobody would have bothered to check that? The waters there are deep enough. It's shallow a few miles from the area, but not there. The water is deep.'

'So what is it? Another magnetic hot spot?'

'No, that's the thing,' Nash said, enjoying telling the story. 'Ship instruments work fine there. In fact, unlike the one in Bermuda, planes can cross through it fine. It's the boats that come to harm.'

'What happens?' Tyler asked.

'They sink. Disappear without a trace. It's a graveyard down there. Wreckage everywhere that has been reclaimed by the waters. Or at least, that's what the stories say.'

'How, though? There must be a reason for it,' Tyler asked.

'Nobody knows,' Liam said, 'although there is a story about the place which I'm sure my father is about to get to.'

'It's a true story. Only thing is nobody believes it, my son included,' Nash snapped.

Tyler waited, reluctant to get involved with the tension between father and son. Both of them sipped their drinks, then Nash went on. 'Back when I was in the Army, we were on a training exercise out there. Our route took us straight through the Devil's Triangle. Of course, back then, I was young and brash. Didn't care for or believe in the stories. We were near the middle of the Triangle when it happened. Explosion from below deck. The boat started to list straight away. Most of us were sleeping, and so by the time we got up, we were already ankle-deep in water.' Nash's good remaining eye took on a vacant glare as he recalled the events. 'We went in the water, forty of us. Some crew went down with the ship. We could see the hole in the hull as it capsized. Something had hit the boat from underneath.'

'What was it?' Tyler asked, drink forgotten.

Nash didn't answer; he stared off into space. 'There was something in the water. Started to take us, those that were left. We didn't know if anyone had sent out a distress call, and there were no landmasses we could get to. All we could do was cling to the wreckage and wait for help that we didn't know was even coming, which was all well and good until we started to die.'

'Sharks?' Tyler asked.

'Just one. A big one. Big enough to sink the boat anyway.'

'Great whites can grow up to twenty feet in these waters. Even so, that's not big enough to sink a boat of that size. You said you had forty men on board.'

'Fifty. Forty went into the water, the rest I'm guessing went down with the ship or couldn't get out.'

'Fifty men, so you'd be talking about a boat that was what, a hundred and fifty, two hundred feet long? No shark could do that.'

'You don't need to give me the history lesson. I've lived here all my life. I've dived with the whites and I know how big they can get. This thing, though…It was no great white. This thing was seventy feet, maybe even eighty.'

Tyler smirked and was about to laugh it off when he saw Nash was deadly serious. 'That's impossible. Something that big would have been found.'

'Depends on how you consider big,' Nash said.

'What do you mean?'

'To you or me, a seventy-foot shark is big. Scaled up to the size of the ocean, seventy feet is nothing. Hell, some blue whales reach almost a hundred feet in length, and manage to go about their business. The only reason we see those is when they surface to breathe. Sharks, of course, don't need to do that.'

'But people would have seen one.'

'I've seen one,' Nash snapped. 'You ever hear of Megalodon?'

Tyler shook his head.

'It was a shark, identical in almost every way to the modern great white but much bigger. They grew up to seventy feet in length. The official story goes that the last ice age caused them to die out, the cooling of the waters making survival for them impossible. As their prey died, they starved as they were too big and slow to capture the smaller creatures that it would have been forced to feed on, but, we know that story is just not true. Fossilised teeth have been found that date to after the ice age. The Megalodon as a species survived that period.'

'Even so, there wouldn't have been enough food to support something so big. You said so yourself. All the bigger prey died. '

'That's not true either. There was an abundance of whales and other large sea creatures which they could feed on in deeper waters. If you accept the possibility that the colder waters slowed their metabolism so that they didn't have to feed so often, then you have a scenario where these things can exist. True, they primarily hunted in warmer waters, but let's just say the ice age forced them to adapt to colder oceans and live deeper where the whales and sufficient prey lived. It's more than possible.'

'Let's say you're right. You don't have any proof.'

Nash leaned on the bar, the lights casting his face into an ugly shadow-filled wasteland. 'This is my evidence. It did this to me. I saw it up close, so yes, I have my evidence.'

Tyler was confused. The conversation seemed to have gone off track and he had no idea where it was going. 'I don't understand what this has to do with gold,' he said.

Nash did his best attempt at a grin and leaned back out of the harsh light. 'There is a story about a boat, a drug-smuggling vessel that was transporting a shipment of gold to a courier ready to be taken to a foundry and melted down by a local cartel. By all accounts, there was around thirty million dollars' worth of it on board. The story goes that the boat never arrived at the pickup and disappeared without a trace. Some say the people driving the boat were ambushed and the cargo stolen. Others say the guys doing the drop off kept the haul, sold it on the black market and lived as rich men. Some say the cartel took it, killed the crew and claimed it never arrived.'

'Let me guess,' Tyler said. 'Another version of the story is that the boat was sunk by your shark in the Devil's Triangle and took the gold down there with it.'

'Exactly.'

'But nobody can get to it because of this…'

'Megalodon,' Nash said, finishing the sentence and taking a sip of his drink.

'Yeah, this Megalodon,' Tyler repeated.

'You don't believe me.'

'No offence, but it seems a little far-fetched.'

Nash turned to Liam. 'Show him.'

'We don't know this guy, are you sure?'

'Yes, I'm sure. We need another pair of hands to do this. Show him.'

Liam flashed another mistrustful look at Tyler then took an object wrapped in cloth from the bag at his feet. 'You'll have to come over to see it. I can't put this on the bar.'

Tyler was too intrigued not to go look. He slid off his bar stool and stood between the two men staring at the wrapped package in Liam's lap.

'Last week, Liam and I were out doing some spotting on the edge of the Triangle.'

'Spotting?' Tyler repeated.

'For the Megalodon.'

'Oh.'

'Anyway, we see something floating in the water so we go and retrieve it. Turns out to be a flotation balloon just drifting along the surface along with a few pieces of debris from a boat.'

'We don't know that, Dad,' Liam cut in.

'Either way, we came across this and pulled it out of the water. There was one object in the netting under the balloon.' Nash nodded to Liam who unwrapped the cloth.

Tyler drew a breath. The gold bar shimmered under the low-level lighting of the bar, appearing like liquid gold. Part of the bar was damaged and worn and exactly how Tyler would expect it to look if it had been submerged underwater for years. Tyler looked at the two men then at the gold.

'Where did this come from?' Tyler asked, finally remembering to breathe.

'Where do you think?' Nash said. 'Local reports say a boat went missing last week. Two brothers, locals. They went out and didn't come back. The floating wreckage we saw was consistent with the same type of boat they had. My guess is they were looking for the gold and found it.'

'Then what?' Tyler asked.

'Then something found them.'

Tyler couldn't take his eyes off the gold. He didn't believe in the shark story. Something so large was impossible. The gold, however, he did believe in, and it was just a few feet away. He blinked as Liam wrapped it up and slipped it back into his bag.

'So, you interested in helping us?' Nash asked.

Tyler returned to his seat and drained half his beer. 'What do you want me to do?'

Nash leaned closer, licking what remained of his lips as he spoke quietly. 'My body is, for want of a better word, fucked, and I can't physically dive down there anymore. Even if I could, frankly, I'm afraid that I'll come face to face with that thing again. You and Liam will dive down to the ship graveyard in Devil's Triangle, and I'll provide support from the surface. For your efforts, you'll get ten percent of the haul, however much that might be.'

'Ten percent? You tell me there's a monster shark down there and then expect me to risk my life for ten percent. Sorry, not happening.'

Nash frowned and glanced at Liam. 'Looks like I said too much too soon. Alright, how does twenty percent sound? We will provide the boat as well as the equipment we need. I'm talking top of the range sonar, and diving gear with face masks that allow us to talk to each other. We will be in constant communication.'

Tyler wasn't a greedy man, yet he knew this was an opportunity for him to permanently put off returning to his mundane life that he had walked away from so long ago if the story was true. If it wasn't, it was another new experience for him to say he had tried. It was about security, and if it meant he had to accept Nash's ghost stories, then he would.

'Man, you're breaking me here. Twenty-five percent and I won't go any higher.'

Nash had mistaken Tyler processing his thoughts as indecision, and the higher offer made the rest easy. 'Alright, you're on.'

'Good to have you on board,' Nash said, trying again to grin.

'Just one thing,' Tyler said, looking at the two of them. 'No offence, but you don't look like you can afford all this fancy equipment you talked about.'

'We can't, or at least we couldn't,' Nash said, glancing to the bag containing the gold bar. 'I know a guy who will exchange that gold piece there for cash no questions asked. Don't worry, we can afford this little project.'

With far too much information already taken on board and unsure how he even got pulled into the entire thing in the first place, Tyler nodded. 'Alright, then I guess I'm in. What happens next?'

'It's going to take a few days to get everything we need. In the meantime, I don't think I need to tell you how important it is to keep this quiet. Nobody around here thinks the Devil's Triangle is real. We need to keep it that way. We need to go in and out quick and quiet before anything finds us.'

Tyler didn't have to ask what he meant. The fear in his good eye said enough. 'No danger of that. I don't know anyone to tell. Comes with the lifestyle.'

'Good. That's exactly what I thought and why I picked you. Liam will give you the address. Be there on Friday morning.'

He waited until Liam had scribbled the details and passed them across to him.

'Alright, then I guess I'll see you Friday morning,' Tyler said, standing and shoving the address into his pocket.

'In the meantime, do yourself a favour. Learn about the Megalodon. Make sure you read up on it. You need to know what you're going up against. I've got enough blood on my hands and don't need anymore.'

Tyler was going to crack a joke, something to lighten the mood, then saw that Nash was serious. 'Alright, I'll do that. See you

Friday morning.'

Tyler finished his drink, slid off his seat and left the bar, realising the slight beer buzz he had before he started talking to Nash had gone. He was now sober and had a head full of questions and speculation. First and foremost, he needed a drink. Just one. Just to calm the nerves.

CHAPTER SIX

Tyler didn't read about the Megalodon, despite his intentions to do so. Instead, he had gotten drunk and let the demon within him roam free. The Friday morning he was supposed to meet Nash and Liam, he had woken as always on the floor of his motel room, head thundering, body filled with pain and regret at his actions. He had half-convinced himself that the whole story was just the ramblings of a drunk, perhaps a glimpse into his own future if he didn't get control of his habit. The one thing that kept his interest was the gold. Sure enough, there was no guarantee that the bar he had been shown came from the Devil's Triangle, but if it was a ruse, Nash was going to extreme lengths to make it seem real. As he dressed and dry swallowed aspirin to relieve the thunderstorm in his head, he supposed today would tell either way. He would go to the dock and see what happened. If there was no Nash or boat, he would move on with his life. He had learned not to try and predict too much of the future and since leaving his old life behind had become blasé about such things. Grabbing his sunglasses to protect him from his hangover, Tyler grabbed his backpack and set out to see what was going to happen next.

***

The heat of the day was brutal and made Tyler's hangover feel even worse. His skin was soaked with sweat, and angry patches of perspiration had formed under the armpits and down the back of his navy polo shirt. Even so, he risked lifting the sunglasses and propping them on his forehead to look at the vessel in Dock 9.

The seventy-two-foot yacht bobbed in the azure waters, sunlight shimmering off its white hull. The windows to the wheelhouse were blacked out, the entire vessel screaming luxury. Across the bow, painted in pale blue was the ship's name. *The Sonnet*. Tyler stared at it, squinting against the sun and watching Nash and Liam load supplies onto the boat.

Nash saw him and waved a scarred arm. 'You made it.'

Tyler stood agape and thinking how Amy would have loved to have seen such a rare thing. He was lost for words. Nash saw it and laughed, fedora flapping in the breeze. 'You thought I was full of shit, didn't you?' he said as he leaned on the rail around the stern of the boat.

'Yeah, actually I did,' Tyler replied.

'Well, don't just stand there, come on board. We've got work to do.'

Tyler tossed his bag onto the deck at the stern and climbed on board the boat. Everything felt surreal, from the gentle sway of the vessel in its berth to the slightly hops and booze smell coming off Nash as he sorted gear on the deck.

'This must have been expensive.'

'It was,' Nash replied. 'Like I said, I know a guy who didn't ask too many questions. Told him it was for a fishing trip just to be safe.'

Tyler exhaled, doing another slow three-sixty as he took everything in. Nash chuckled as he handed a box of supplies to Liam. 'You're still struggling to take it all in, aren't you?'

Tyler was caught off guard by the directness of the question and was spared having to answer by Nash's laugh as he clapped him on the back. 'Don't worry about it, the story is pretty unbelievable, isn't it?'

Tyler nodded, the growing feeling of unease in his gut becoming harder to ignore. Nash checked his watch, then squinted up at the sun. 'Well, maybe we should be on our way. Weather looks clear at least, so that's in our favour. I want to do this during daylight hours.'

Tyler nodded. Now he was standing on the boat and everything Nash had told him was turning out to be true, he couldn't help but think about the shark story he had been told. He still didn't think it was possible, but he knew the more time he spent with Nash and the closer they got to their destination, the idea would grow and fester in his mind.

'Hey,' Liam said, wiping the sweat from his forehead with a muscular forearm and then picking up another box of supplies. 'Any chance of a little help here?'

'Yeah, sorry,' Tyler said, grabbing another one of the boxes and following Liam into the galley. Within the hour, they were underway, Nash piloting the boat, Liam engrossed in his phone, earphones in so he didn't have to make conversation. Tyler stood out on the back deck by the transom, staring at the white wake left by the boat as it moved into deeper waters. As he watched the land receded into a hazy smudge on the horizon, he found himself thinking about the Megalodon, now only half sure it couldn't be real.

***

The initial excitement had waned. The day was hot and sticky, and because of the hangover, the sun wasn't something Tyler wanted to become too acquainted with, especially with the constant drone of the engine making his headache worse by the hour. Liam had disappeared below decks to his cabin to sleep, and so Tyler joined Nash at the wheel, watching the bow of the boat slice through the gorgeous blue waters. The wheelhouse was wood panelled. In addition to the controls to drive the boat, there were other devices propped on the console. A bank of CCTV monitors displayed blue standby screens. Beside these was a radar screen, their vessel marked in red in the centre of the display. To Nash's right was the fish finder, its screen a kaleidoscope of ridges and valleys as the under-hull-mounted camera mapped the sea floor. Nash glanced at him as he entered the wheelhouse, then turned back towards the water.

'How are you finding the trip? Been sick yet?' Nash asked. He was like a different person now that he was away from the prying eyes of society. He had shed the hat and abundance of layers and was wearing knee-length cargo shorts, a loose white shirt and brown sandals. Tyler tried not to stare at the horrific map of scars on his body, the damage even more visible in the harsh light of day.

'I'm good, I've managed to keep everything on board for now,' he said, turning his attention back to the ocean.

Nash chuckled. 'You're lucky it's smooth going. If the seas were rough and we were vaulting over six-foot swells, you might be saying something else.'

Tyler approached, standing beside Nash. 'This looks like a lot of equipment.'

'State of the art. The very best.' He nodded towards the blue screened CCTV monitors. 'Those are for the live drone feeds. When we reach the Devil's Triangle, we'll send down the remote control drones. They are attached to the surface by fibre-optic tethers, which was what you and Liam were bringing on board earlier. Because we don't know what's down there, the plan is to send those in first and scan the area to see what we're dealing with.'

'Yeah? I thought you were just going to put me on the end of a fishing line to bait your shark.'

Tyler meant it as a joke, but Nash wasn't amused. 'You didn't do the research, did you?' Nash said, staring straight ahead.

'I...no. I didn't.'

'I thought not. If you did, you wouldn't be so...relaxed.'

'Look, I'm sorry, I don't mean anything by it, it's just...It's a stretch.'

Nash shrugged. 'I can't blame you. Even my own son doesn't believe it. Like you, he half-thinks I'm a crazy old man and half-thinks there might be some money to be made, so he tolerates my rambling.'

'Look, it's not—'

'It doesn't matter. People thinking like that isn't new to me. You should prepare yourself though for me to be proved right. I've seen what's down there, and I know what we have to potentially face.'

'Look, I'll be straight with you, I'm not sold on your shark story. I don't doubt you were attacked, the evidence of that is plain to see. My doubt is your account of the size of the shark. You know, from so low in the water when you were cold and scared, it would be easy for the brain to scale this creature up to something monstrous. I didn't read up on the Megalodon because I don't believe it's down there. Sharks roam, I know that much. It's unlikely they would stick around in one place for years to protect some gold that they won't have any awareness of. Now if we can get down there, get the gold you say is on the sea floor and get back to shore without any more shark talk, I'd appreciate it.'

Nash stared at him with his one good eye as if seeing Tyler for the first time. 'Alright, if that's the way you want it, that's how it will be. I won't mention it again. You're the one who will be down there, not me.'

'Exactly. Your son will be, too. I don't think he'd appreciate hearing this either.'

'You say it like I hope that thing is down there.'

'That's how it sounds,' Tyler said, curious to see where the conversation went. 'Seems to me it's important for you to prove us wrong. Even more than the finding the gold.'

'That's not the case. I know what I saw. You think you're the first to say it was because I was scared or because how close I was to it?' Nash grimaced. 'No, I know what I saw. And I'm no fool. I know about these creatures. I've read about them, obsessed over them for the last thirty years. I'm not so stupid to think they are guarding their gold. What I do think this Megalodon is guarding is its territory. These creatures were very territorial animals. The area we're going to is shallow, but it sits on the edge of a deep water chasm frequented by whale pods. I suspect those whales form the basis of the diet for the Megalodon. Why should it leave the area? Its food regularly comes directly to it. It's a perfect setup.'

'Wait, I know a bit about whales. They are buoyant. Wouldn't the remains float to the surface and wash up somewhere? Surely, if someone found a whale carcass that one of these mega sharks have taken a bite out of, then someone would have found one by now.'

Nash chuckled and altered the boat's course slightly.

'What's so funny?' Tyler asked.

'How little you know about these things. You ask why the remains wouldn't show up. Let me answer that for you. When these things have finished feeding, there are no remains left to surface. Nothing goes to waste.' Nash walked across the wheelhouse to a cupboard. He opened it and took out some books, handing them to Tyler. 'We've got a ways to go yet. It might be worth doing a little reading just so you at least know what to do if this isn't a figment of my imagination.'

Tyler leafed through the books. They were well-thumbed volumes about prehistoric predators, shark behaviour, and the Megalodon. Tyler considered another sarcastic remark then decided to keep it to himself. He didn't want to be thrown overboard. Instead, he tucked the books under his arm. 'Fine, I'll take a look. If nothing else, I might learn a few things.'

'You do that.'

Tyler went to leave, then stopped and turned back to Nash. 'Just one thing. When we get there, to this Devil's Triangle, what if someone disturbs us there. A passing vessel or the Coast Guard or something. What do we say?'

'No danger of that. No shipping lanes go where we're going. It's essentially out in the middle of nowhere.' Nash took a dog-eared map and rolled it out on the console. On the map was a crudely drawn triangle in an area of open ocean. 'This is where we're heading,' Nash said. 'The shipping lanes as you can see are nowhere even close. They used to run through here up until the seventies. All the shipping lanes now run further north. We'll be undisturbed.'

'What about those?' Tyler said, pointing to the two small islands to within the triangle.

'Uninhabited. Mostly rock outcrops with a little vegetation. Waters there are shallow. Thousands of years ago, those two little islands were part of one large landmass. Now those two little islands are all that remains of it. The rest is underwater.'

'If it's shallow, maybe that's why all these boats are sinking.'

Nash shook his head. 'No. It's only shallow in that small area around the islands. The rest of the surrounding ocean is as you expect. It's deep. This isn't a case of ships running aground. This is something else.'

'Alright, you clearly know more about this than me. I just wanted to make sure we didn't get into any trouble.'

'Unless you think seagulls will call the Coast Guard, we're safe,' Nash replied.

Tyler stared at the map, frown etched on his brow. He could feel Nash staring at him.

'What are you thinking?' Nash asked.

'Just that with this being so remote, if anything goes wrong, we'll be far from help.'

Nash nodded. 'Which is why I've taken all the necessary precautions. Here, let me show you.'

Nash rolled up the map and put it beside the console then turned back to the monitors that had been installed. 'Alright, here's how this will work. You see the monitors here?' Nash pointed to the blue standby screens.

'Yeah.'

'Well, each screen is linked to one of the manta drones we brought on board.'

'You just told me that. They are going down first, right?'

Nash nodded. 'That's not all. Once we've located what we are looking for, the manta drones will be positioned in a circular formation around you and Liam. As you load up the gold, I'll monitor the live feeds from the drone cameras. The feed is super high resolution and also has night vision and thermal imaging. I'll be monitoring those from the surface and keeping in constant contact with you from the surface. I know you don't believe it, but I do, and I want to be sure the both of you are safe.'

'You can pilot all those drones by yourself?'

'They are designed to have adjustable buoyancy, so essentially, once they are in position, I can adjust the levels and the mantas will just sit there until I move them. They will need small tweaks to account for currents, but I can handle it. Think of it like spinning plates. As long as I keep moving from one to the other to adjust them, it will be fine.'

'Let's hope the units work as they should.'

Nash snorted. 'Don't let the fact that my hand is the way it is fool you. I was a good engineer before this happened to me and I still do alright now. I've personally set up each manta ahead of the dive. They will work.'

'And what about the gold? How will we find that? Looking at the map you just showed me, this Devil's Triangle is huge.'

'We're heading back to the location where we found the flotation balloons and the gold bar. Seems like a good place to me. There was still a fair bit of surface debris, too, so it stands to reason that the gold was found in the general vicinity.'

'And how will we get the gold to the surface if we find any?'

'Seems to me the flotation balloon idea is a good one. We've brought some with us. Any more questions?'

Tyler could see he was getting on Nash's nerves, and decided it would be best to leave him alone. 'No, that's all, thanks. I'm going to head below and look at these books.'

'Study them, Tyler. They could save your life.'

Tyler left the wheelhouse, books in hand. The closer they got to their destination, the more he wanted to know about Nash's shark theory. Just to be safe.

CHAPTER SEVEN

The Devil's Triangle. 100 miles off the coast of Australia.

'We're here,' Nash said as he put the boat into neutral, letting it ebb with the gentle tide. They had been sailing for almost eight hours and the sun was starting to dip towards the horizon, turning the ocean into an expanse of fire. Nash walked out onto the rear deck, squinting against the sun as he surveyed the water. Tyler joined him. He had expected to see something. A marker or some other landmark to show that they were in the right place. He turned in a slow circle, scanning the waves, nervous that they were so far away from land.

'It's quiet,' Tyler said as the boat creaked and swayed on the tide.

'Yeah, nothing out here but us now.'

'What are those?' Tyler said, pointing at two rocky outcrops on the horizon.

'Those islands I told you about on the map. See what I mean about them being too far away to be the cause of the sinking ships?' Nash said. He was sweating, his eyes darting over the surface of the water.

Tyler walked to the stern, staring into the blue depths. Now he was there, everything seemed much more real. 'Do you really think it's down there?'

Nash grinned and joined Tyler at the stern. 'Did some reading, I take it? Made you a believer now.'

'I was talking about the gold, not the shark.' He expected Nash to go into another one of his sermons, but he was too distracted. He was flexing his good hand as he stared at the water. 'You know, I've been waiting to get to this stage for so long, and now that I'm here, I can't stop shaking. Hopefully, we'll find something otherwise, this will have been a very expensive wasted trip.'

Liam joined them on deck, already wearing his wetsuit. 'You better get changed. We're losing daylight.'

Tyler nodded, unable to hide the nerves that were setting in. Now, more than ever, he desperately wanted a few drinks. The inner demon was stirring and he wondered if Nash had brought any alcohol on board.

'I'll get the drones ready,' Nash said. 'The two of you will have to get them into the water for me, my arm…' He trailed off, good hand still flexing with nerves.

Tyler felt like he was running on autopilot, somehow detached from reality. The closer he got to actually entering the water, the more aware he was that he didn't know the people he was with and that he was trusting his life to strangers. He still couldn't accept that there was a giant monster beneath the waves, and he had seen enough of Nash to know he was slightly unhinged. There was always the 'what if' though. After all, even crazy people were right sometimes and he couldn't shake that off. With it in his mind, Tyler went below deck to change and maybe see if he could find a bottle of something to take the edge off his nerves.

II

Liam was lowering the last of the drones into the ocean as Tyler returned in his black and red wetsuit. It was a snug fit, his belly straining against the material. He had been unable to find any alcohol which had put him into a bad mood. It made him aware just how big a problem he had developed and knew he needed to fix it. Not yet, though, when there was so much stress about the pending dive. With the growing dark, the ocean no longer looked gorgeous and relaxing. Instead, it looked like the most inhospitable, uninviting place he had ever seen.

'You okay there, big man? Not lost your nerve, have you?'

Tyler looked at Liam, wishing he had a little of the same cocky confidence. 'I'm fine.'

'Good, because we can't afford any mistakes down there. For the record, I wanted to do this alone but my dad insisted we bring someone else in. Just do as I tell you and everything will be fine.'

'Good luck giving me instructions under water,' Tyler grunted, deciding he preferred the sulky, quiet version of Nash's son. Liam shook his head and crossed the deck to the scuba gear, then stared at Tyler. 'Come over here, let me teach you a little something.'

Ignoring the goading tone, Tyler joined Liam by the equipment. He glanced at Nash to see if he was going to say anything to his son, but he was preoccupied calibrating the underwater mantas, lost in the controls and array of screens in front of him.

'Hey, you listening?' Liam said.

'Yeah, I'm listening.'

'These are full-face scuba masks. They pull over your head like a hood and are vacuum sealed. Take a look.' Liam handed Tyler the facemask. It was a black neoprene hood with the regulator built into the full-face Lexan mask. The rectangular window would give excellent views of the surrounding ocean, and calmed Tyler's nerves a little at the thought of having to bite down on a regulator for the entire duration of the dive.

'Nice, this is impressive.'

'There's a microphone and speaker inside so we'll be able to communicate when we're under. Air gauge will attach to your wrist as normal. Both air tanks are full, though, so I wouldn't expect it to be a problem.'

Tyler looked out at the ever approaching night. 'What about visibility? How will we see?'

Tyler pointed to the mask. 'See there around the edge of the mask? High-power LED lights. Better than any handheld torch. Also, the boat has powerful lights underneath the hull. My dad will illuminate as far as he can from the surface. With both combined, we'll see better than if we were in full daylight.'

'And what if, uh, what if something goes wrong. If there is an emergency.'

'You mean if you see the Meg?'

'No, of course not,' Tyler said, hoping his lie wasn't too transparent.

Liam snorted. 'We've got the Zodiac in the water by the boat. If you get into trouble down there or there are any other issues, we can be on it and away from the danger quick as you like. Good enough?''

Tyler nodded. His nerves had already started to recede. He had gone from expecting a horrific, claustrophobic descent in near darkness to facing a well-lit comfortable swim to the seafloor to see if Nash was crazy or right about the gold.

'You two ready?' Nash asked, grinning at them as he activated the exterior lights on the boat, throwing an eerie blue-green halo around the hull.

'Yeah,' Tyler said, unsure if he believed it or not. He wasn't about to show he was afraid. The beast called male pride kept his emotions hidden. 'Let's do it,' he added, aware of how dry his throat was and wishing again for that drink. He watched as Liam pulled the neoprene mask over his head and did the same, his hearing muffled by the material against his ears. There was a strange sense of calm as he became isolated in his own bubble, the faceplate separating him from the world. He inhaled, the clean oxygen filtering into his mask.

'Hey, can you hear me?'

Tyler looked to Liam, his electronic-filtered voice coming through a small speaker in the face panel of the mask. Tyler nodded, wishing he could slow his heart rate.

'You need to speak so we can check we have reception,' Liam said, the irritation unmistakeable.

'Yeah, I hear you fine, uh, roger.'

'Alright, I got you. You don't need to say roger or over and out. Just talk normally.'

'Alright, sorry.'

'Forget it. Just a couple of things to run through before we go down. At the bottom edge of your facemask, do you see an LED strip going left to right, red graduating to blue?'

'I see it,' Tyler said.

'Good. That's your air gauge. Both tanks are full and we will be back to the surface before we get anywhere close to running out of air, but I thought it best to tell you what it was.'

'Got it,' Tyler said the tempo of his heart finally starting to slow to something resembling normality.

'Dad, are you hearing us okay?'

'Got you both loud and clear,' Nash said over the speaker. Tyler could see him settled in at the control console for the drones, headset over his scarred skull. 'Mantas have scanned the area and it's clear. Nothing down there. I do see some wrecks down there though so you both might want to get into the water. Sooner the better.'

Liam walked to the transom, sitting on the rear of the boat and putting on his flippers. Tyler joined him, the muffled sounds of the world giving him no comfort. He sat next to Liam, unable to resist a glance into the artificially lit depths. He put on his own flippers, wondering if his hands would shake and pleased to see that they were steady. Liam stood and turned to Tyler. 'You ready?'

Tyler nodded, then remembered he was supposed to speak. 'Yeah. Good to go.'

'Alright. Then just remember to follow my lead. I'm pretty sure you've never done this before but my dad wants you out there to help. Just do as I say and everything will be fine. Got it?'

'Yeah, I got it.'

'Then let's go.'

'What about the flotation balloon?'

'We don't need it yet. This trip is just so we can go look and see if there is anything down there. If there is, we'll come back for the balloon.' Liam walked to the ladder set into the transom and climbed down it, his feet inches from the waterline. He folded his arms across his chest and pushed off backwards, disappearing into the water, his mass becoming a blurred black shape below the waterline. Tyler stared at the water, his chest drumming its higher tempo again.

'You coming or not?' Liam's voice said in Tyler's facemask. Although he couldn't see him, Tyler could imagine the arrogant look on his face.

'Yeah, on my way' he said, also climbing the ladder. He looked across the deck at Nash, who was watching him intently, one good eye judging and curious. Then, with less finesse than Liam had managed, Tyler dropped into the water, ready to face whatever waited for him beyond.

#

Fear became secondary to wonder as Tyler kicked in ten feet of water. The lights from the boat illuminated his world, microscopic life drifting and undulating on the currents. Liam was ten feet below and waiting. Tyler couldn't see his face but thought he was probably getting impatient. Tyler angled towards him, reluctant to leave the light generated by the boat.

'I thought you'd lost your nerve,' Liam said as Tyler fell in alongside him.

The jibes were making Tyler angry, but he managed not to react, knowing it wasn't the time or place. The younger version of himself would have responded with sarcasm or aggression, but he wasn't about to get drawn into petty squabbles, as they were now in a hostile environment. Instead, he focused on his surroundings, the darkness swallowing them as they made their way deeper. He saw Liam activate his exterior facemask light and realised he didn't know how to do the same.

'Hey, uh, how do I do that? The light,' he said, hating that he was so needy.

'The cuff on your wrist. Turn the dial.'

Tyler complied, turning the dial on the Velcro cuff and feeling better as the darkness was expelled by the array of LED lights in his facemask. He hoped to see fish darting around his field of vision, but instead saw only the water and the drifting tide of microscopic life within it. There was a sense of serenity beneath the surface that banished his nerves even though he was aware of just how vast his surroundings were. He was a tiny creature in a huge and thriving ecosystem, something which was both humbling and terrifying at the same time.

'How are you both doing?'

Nash's voice disturbed the crushing silence and reminded Tyler that he was there to do a job.

'We're fine. How is it looking up there?' Liam replied.

'All good up here. Drones are with you in a perimeter

formation.'

Tyler looked around, surprised to see the drones so close. He had been completely unaware of their presence and was impressed with how silently they were able to move through the water.

'How is visibility?' Nash asked.

'Not great,' Tyler said, unsure if it was him who was being addressed. 'I still don't understand why we couldn't wait until daylight to do this.'

'I told you already, it wouldn't have made too much difference. Sunlight will only reach so far. Just relax and focus. You should be seeing the bottom soon.'

'There it is,' Liam said.

Tyler couldn't see it at first, just the black waters and microscopic life. He was about to ask what he should be looking for when the sandy bottom melted out of the darkness below him.

'Dad, are you seeing this?' Liam said, for once without attitude or arrogance.

'Yeah, I see it.'

Tyler could see it, too. He had expected to see a little bit of floating debris at best, maybe some man-made rubbish that had been tossed into the ocean and forgotten. Instead, he found himself looking at what he could only describe as a boat graveyard. There was a barnacle-encrusted fishing trawler to his left on its side, half-buried in the soft sand. Ahead, the skeletal ribs were all that remained of a larger vessel. The more Tyler looked, the more he saw in the widening debris field. 'This is incredible,' he whispered, more to himself than anyone else.

'Hang on,' Nash said. 'I'll power up the drone lights.'

Seconds later, the full scale of the debris field was fully illuminated as Nash activated each drone's powerful spotlights, banishing the darkness and illuminating their surroundings.

'Jesus, just look at it,' Liam muttered.

Tyler could think of no way to reply. He licked his lips, aware of just how dry they were. The extra visibility exposed more wreckage. The shattered bow of a trawler. Rusting sheets of steel panelling on the ground which were teeming with rusticles as nature claimed the man-made waste. More than anything, they could see the gold. The powerful lights making the seabed glow like fire as the gold bars scattered across the debris field became visible.

'You were right, Dad. There's gold down here. A lot of it.' Liam was breathless and excited, and Tyler couldn't help but feel the same way.

'There are so many wrecks down here,' Tyler said, his voice sounding strange in the enclosed environment of his facemask.

'You're telling me. I never imagined there would be so many.'

It was the first time Liam had been civil with him, and Tyler hoped that the hostile attitude had been some kind of initiation and done with, or, alternatively, that the sheer thrill of discovery had made him forget the sizeable chip on his shoulder.

'This is going to take a few trips. There is so much gold down here we can't bring it up in one trip.' The excitement in Liam's voice was hard to ignore. Tyler was staring at the wrecks, some still nothing more than shadows on the periphery of the spotlights, hulking bones yet to be discovered. Tyler was staring at the outer edge when something caught his eye. He flicked his head around, staring into the distance and recalling the landscape as it had been. He was certain he had seen something move, and now one of the large shapes on the edge of the reach of the lights wasn't there anymore. His instinct said there was definitely an object, something large and tapered at one end like—

The nose of a shark

—a bow of a large vessel, but now there was nothing. He supposed he could have been mistaken or shifted position and had lost his bearings, but even as the thoughts occurred, he knew neither of those things had happened.

'Hey, you helping or what?' Liam said as he kicked towards the seabed.

'Yeah, sorry I just…I thought I saw something.'

'Saw what? What did you see?' The desperation in Nash's voice made Tyler even more uncomfortable.

'Nothing, it's…nothing,' he muttered as the blood pounded around his body thick in his temples. He willed himself to calm down and tried to convince himself that he had made a mistake. The problem with trying to do that was that he knew he hadn't. He had seen something out there, something large that was now gone. He—

'Hey. If you want a cut of this gold, you better come help me.' Liam, it seemed, had rediscovered the shoulder chip he had lost and was now close to the floor, kicking in place and looking back at him where he floated twenty feet above him in the open water.

Exposed.

That thought scared him, and so instead of following his instinct to kick to the surface as fast as he could, he descended, joining Liam on the debris-covered seabed. Now separated by just a few feet, Tyler could see how angry his fellow diver was.

'You need to get your shit together and help me. You're no use just gawping at the scenery.'

'Sorry,' Tyler said, resisting the urge to do a full three-sixty and look at his surroundings. Every passing second raised his anxiety levels and made him long for the surface. He pushed those thoughts aside and tried to focus on the task at hand. 'What do you need me to do?'

'We need to survey this area to see how much gold there is. I didn't expect it to be even here, never mind in such large amounts. We need to be efficient in getting it to the surface I—' Liam paused and looked past Tyler, his brow furrowed.

'What is it? What's wrong?' Tyler said, joining him in staring out into the black waters.

'Nothing I…I thought I saw something.'

'Saw what? What did you see?' Nash blurted into their microphones. For once, Tyler didn't mind. He wanted to know the answer to the question also.

'It's nothing, I thought I saw something move that's all. Trick of the light.'

Tyler opened his mouth to speak, intending to tell Liam he too had seen something and to suggest they head back to the surface when he spoke again. His voice was an octave higher than normal.

'Look, it's nothing, alright? I made a mistake. Let's just do our fucking jobs.'

And so they did.

They moved around the debris field, marking the locations of the gold by the GPS tracking system attached to their wrists. Each coordinate would be relayed to the surface where Nash could make a virtual map of the gold and make a plan to retrieve it. For Tyler, it was only pride and the fact he didn't want to see the smug look on Liam's face that he remained beneath the surface. He was trying to distract himself with the tedious work of marking the locations of the gold and telling himself that he was about to become a very rich man when Nash's voice crackled over the speaker.

'Stop moving, both of you.'

Tyler didn't immediately acknowledge the instruction, or why it would have been said until he saw the shark swimming towards them with casual grace. Tyler froze, heart thundering as he watched the majestic creature draw near.

'It's huge,' he whispered, more to himself than in communication.

'It's just a great white,' Liam said, the arrogance becoming something Tyler was finding harder and harder to ignore. Liam was still working, cataloguing samples.

'He's right,' Nash said, sounding almost disappointed. 'Looks like she's a big one, though. Fifteen footer.'

Tyler wasn't sure about that. From his exposed position, it seemed much bigger. Its massive head swayed as it swam over them.

'Relax, he's not interested in us,' Liam said as the shark increased its speed and disappeared into the dark. Tyler looked across at him and was about to say he was heading back to the surface when he saw one of the sunken boats in the distance move towards them. He blinked, and there was the split second realisation that it wasn't a boat that was moving, but something else.

'Jesus Christ, it's real,' Tyler muttered. Liam, too, was frozen in place and staring at the giant making its way towards them. It was something beyond either of their ability to comprehend. Tyler had considered the white shark as big before he saw the Megalodon. The creatures head was as large as the front of a school bus, its jaws partially open to allow the seawater to flow through as it drifted through the water. Its skin was a brownish grey, and as it came closer, Tyler could see that it was pocked with scars from a lifetime of battles. On its flank, just above the enormous dorsal fin was an old splintered remains of a wooden harpoon.

'Nash, what do we do?' Tyler asked, his throat dry as he watched the immense predator come out of the gloom. 'Nash, can you hear me?'

'Don't do anything. Don't react. Don't move. Put your back against the nearest hull and wait.'

'Wait? Are you insane?'

'He's likely not interested in you. He seems curious about the drones.'

'It's coming towards us, Dad,' Liam said, the arrogant man replaced by a frightened boy.

'Do as I say. Don't move, and for Christ's sake, stay calm. It will sense your fear.'

'Sense our fear? It's not a damn psychic,' Liam blurted, close to losing control.

'He's right,' Tyler said, recalling the parts of the book Nash had given him. 'Sharks sense electromagnetic pulses in their prey when they are distressed. You don't want this thing to see you as a viable meal.'

'Meal? That thing would swallow us whole.'

'Then do as I say and don't move,' Nash hissed, causing the microphone to crackle.

The Megalodon cruised past them, the pressure as it displaced the water pushing them back against the hull of the sunken boat. Tyler had never experienced terror in such a pure form. It surged through him, his stomach light and rolling as he waited to see if he was about to die. The giant shark opened its mouth, exposing its nine-inch serrated teeth, then, just as Tyler was sure he was about to be devoured, the Megalodon changed direction, more interested in the drones that were surrounding the scene as it played out.

Tyler turned towards Liam just in time to see him disappear as he swam for the surface. 'Hey, what are you doing? We were told to stay still,' he hissed as he watched the Megalodon drift towards the drones. If Liam heard him, he didn't respond. He was already disappearing from view into the dark. The Megalodon had turned away from him now, leaving him on the edge of following Liam or doing as Nash had said. In the end, his instinct told him to flee, and so he kicked his legs, trying to remain calm as he ascended in pursuit of Liam.

'What are you doing? I told you both to stay still damn it!' Nash grunted through the mic. Tyler, like Liam, failed to respond. The riches hidden on the sea floor could stay there. He didn't care about it anymore. All he wanted to do was to breathe fresh air and leave the domain of the monster shark, never to return. As he left the safety of the light cast by the drones, he was incredibly aware of everything going on around him. The immense isolation, the resistance of the black waters against his skin, the presence of the prehistoric giant that could, if it so chose, end his existence with little effort.

'Damn you two, you're ruining everything,' Nash bellowed through the speakers. Tyler risked looking down into the artificial pool of light cast by the drones. The Megalodon was agitated and charged one of the drones. The manta moved toward it in response. There was an immense explosion as the shark's jaws clamped down on the drone, sending it reeling away. The other drones were moving closer to the shark, but Tyler was aware his pace was slowing and he was desperate to get back to the surface. He turned his attention to the opaque mass above him and swam into is, legs tiring as he kicked towards the surface.

He came up twenty feet off the port side of the boat. Liam was already climbing the ladder on the transom. Tyler swam for the ladder, wanting to get there before father and son decided to leave without him. He was exhausted, his legs heavy from the exertion. He gripped the steel rung, pulling himself out of the water, his feet scrambling for purchase on the wet rungs. On the deck, Nash was pacing, clearly agitated. Liam was on all fours, breathing hard.

'What the hell was that?' Tyler said as he yanked off his mask and tossed it across the deck. 'You fucking left me down there.'

Nash glared at them both then stared at the console which showed the red blip approaching. 'You don't know what you've done. It followed you, you assholes, it followed—'

The boat exploded from the rear, splintering into fragments as the prehistoric missile slammed into it from the rear. Tyler was launched into the air, arms flailing, unaware that he was screaming. An image from a nature programme he had seen some years earlier popped into his mind about killer whales and the way they would toss seals into the air before they killed them. There was no time to develop the thought, because gravity had taken over and he impacted the water, hitting the surface hard and taking an impulsive breath, he swallowed in a mouthful of sea water and starting to choke, slipping beneath the surface as debris started to rain down around him for the destroyed boat. He couldn't breathe, couldn't swim or keep his head above the surface.

This is it. This is where I die.

The thought didn't worry him as much as he thought for the simple reason that this way was better. Better than suffering in the jaws of the monster shark which was punishing them for daring to encroach on its territory. Tyler slipped under, enveloped in the black calm of unconsciousness as the chaos and destruction continued around him.

II

Nash was, in that instant, transported back thirty years. He tread water, coughing and blinking his good eye as he watched the boat begin to list to at the stern. He knew this scene. It had played out in his mind hundreds of times. The chill bite of the water, the feeling of the eternal depths below him, the groan as the boat began its journey to its final resting place. And of course, the shark. The demon from his nightmares come to life in the real world for the second time. Its massive head was out of the water, snapping at the debris spilling from the boat. Nash was mesmerised. Even though he never doubted its existence, to see it in front of him again in all its horrific glory was something beyond his ability to comprehend. Like him, it wore scars on its body, a mark of a creature that survived against all odds. It seemed they were not too dissimilar. He wondered how it would feel when it took him. If it would hurt, if he would be aware of those huge serrated teeth shredding his flesh, or if his life would just cease to exist, snuffed out in an instant. There was no fear, no conscious thought of survival, just peace that at last the lifetime of fear would be over. The shark would finish what it started all those years ago.

'Dad, come on,' Liam screamed from somewhere behind him. Nash ignored it. He watched the beast, his nemesis, the monster that had plagued both every waking moment and his nightmares, too, as it attacked the boat again, hurrying its journey to join the others in the graveyard beneath the surface.

'Dad!' Liam screamed. Nash blinked and whatever spell that had transfixed him was broken. He looked over his shoulder at his son, who was already out of the water and in the Zodiac. He had the unconscious Tyler under the arms and was struggling to pull him out of the water. 'Swim, you've got to swim over and help me. I can't pull him out on my own.'

Nash heard him, but in his mind, he was thirty years younger. 'Huddle together. Keep still and in a pack,' someone had shouted. Too young to argue and too afraid to wonder if the command was right or wrong, the young Nash had complied. They all did. Even when the water turned red and they were picked off in threes and fours.

'Dad, goddamn it,' Liam screamed, snapping Nash back to the present. 'I'm letting him go, I'm coming to get you.'

'No,' Nash screamed, paddling towards the Zodiac. 'Don't do that.' He swam to the Zodiac, all the time waiting for the beast to claim him, and in doing so, close the thread of that particular story. Nash arrived at the side of the zodiac, the yellow inflatable bobbing on the surface. Nash tried to climb out, but his broken body was too weak for him to pull himself over onto the boat.

'Let me drop him. He's unconscious anyway, it will be quick for him. Let me help you.'

Nash ignored him. He wrapped his good arm around Tyler's legs and pushed as Liam pulled, together the two of them able to get the dead weight out of the water. Nash risked a glance behind him, hoping to see the shark, but it had gone along with the boat, which had slipped beneath the waves.

'Pull me out,' he grunted, his legs tiring. Liam grabbed him and pulled, but Nash's clothes were waterlogged, the ocean reluctant to give up its grip. Nash could sense the shark below him. He imagined he could feel the pull of displaced water as the Megalodon circled, ready to launch its attack. It was this pure fear which made his adrenaline surge, and with a roar of defiance, he managed to swing one leg over onto the nine foot inflatable, Liam underneath him. They sat there floating in the debris field, both of them unable to do anything but stare as the six foot, slate-coloured dorsal fin broke the surface. Nash stared at it as it circled the inflatable, the current made by its wake pulling them into a slow rotation so that the fin was never out of eye contact. Once again, Nash went into a trance-like state, staring at the creature he referred to as his nemesis, any doubt he had imagined or overcompensated for the size of the creature dispelled. The Megalodon's head broke the surface, a triangular wedge of horrific proportions. Nash had heard about this in white sharks who would lift their head out of the water to spot their prey. The shark stared at them with its black, lifeless eye, and Nash's milky eye looked right back at it, the sense of helplessness in the presence of a superior predator complete and undisputed. Time lost all sense of meaning. For Nash, nothing else existed. He wondered if the shark remembered if it was able to recall the last time they faced off. The moment was broken when Liam pulled the chord for the engine, the outboard motor spluttering to life with a whine as the water churned.

'No, don't do that!' Nash screamed, but it was already too late. The vibrations of the motor reached the Megalodon in seconds, causing it to go into attack mode. Liam swung the boat away from the shark, his eyes wild with fear as the Zodiac bounced over the waves. On the horizon, almost lost as the last of the daylight faded, was the shape of one of the small islands jutting out of the water. Liam aimed for it, powering the Zodiac at full speed. Nash was mesmerised, watching the immense dorsal fin slice through the water and closing the distance to them.

'We're going to make it,' Leam screamed, his hair flapping in the wind, voice high and shrill. 'We're going to be fine, we're going to—' He was cut off and the lightweight raft was hit from underneath and launched into the air, it's passengers with it. Before he made contact with the water and faced the certain death that awaited them, Nash found a split second to be jealous of Tyler. At least he was unconscious and would feel no pain. Any further thought was cut off as he hit the water and waited for his turn to die.

PART TWO: SURVIVOR

DAY 1

Tyler coughed, rolling onto his side and spitting up seawater onto the rocks. His face was hot, blistered by the sun as waves broke against the formation he was sprawled on, showering him with spray. He had no idea where he was, nor any recollection of how he arrived there. He sat up, squinting at the ocean, then over his shoulder. Nash and Liam sat further up the shale 'beach' before the small island transformed into boulders. Island, was, in fact, too strong a word. Tyler turned back to the ocean, then squinted at the gorgeous blue sky.

'You're alive,' Nash said from behind him.

Tyler didn't answer. He was trying to recall what had happened, to piece together how he had come to be on the island, but his brain was fuzzy and he couldn't figure it out. 'What happened?' he asked, throat dry.

'What does it look like?' Liam said. He was sitting a little further away with his back to a large jagged boulder.

Tyler looked again at their surroundings. It was essentially a large mound of rocks. No vegetation that he could see and, more worryingly, no sign of their boat. 'I don't remember anything after I hit the water.'

Liam and Nash glanced at each other. 'Nothing at all?' Nash asked.

'No.'

'That will be the shock, I expect,' Nash said. Tyler stood and looked at their bleak surroundings, then noticed that Nash was injured.

'What happened to your leg?'

Nash glanced at it stretched out in front of him the ugly wound deep in his calf starting to discolour at the edges. The rock underneath it soaked with blood.

'I had the Zodiac in the water just in case the shark decided to attack. I knew you didn't believe me, but that didn't mean I wasn't ready.'

'Zodiac?'

'Inflatable motor boat. The reason we're all still alive. Anyway, Liam and me got to the boat, saw you floating in the water, and fished you out just as our shark realised we were trying to get away. Son of a bitch chased us, cut us off from heading back to land and so this was the next nearest spot. It led us here then launched us out of the water a few hundred yards from this fucking rock. The Zodiac was destroyed, but we were lucky enough to be in the shallows so he couldn't give chase. He's still out there, though. He's angry and waiting for us.'

Tyler glanced out at the water, sunlight shimmering off its surface, then turned back to Nash.

'Anyway, when he knocked the Zodiac from under us, we went in the water and I cut my leg on the rocks. It's deep and needs stitches but nothing I can do about it now apart from try to keep it clean.'

'Alright, so what's the plan? Do we wait until someone comes to save us?'

Nash and Liam glanced at each other again. 'You don't seem to understand our situation here,' Nash said, shifting position and wincing in pain. 'Nobody is coming here for us. Nobody knows we're here.'

Tyler grinned, then realised it was no joke. 'Are you kidding me? The world connected the way it is, it's impossible to get lost or go missing. Of course someone will find us.'

Nash shook his head. 'Nobody knows we're out here. We kept it quiet for obvious reasons. You, of course, are also off the grid. This rock is miles from any shipping lane. The nearest land is a hundred miles away.'

'Maybe we can signal a passing plane. Light a fire or something to get their attention.'

Nash looked around him. 'How? With what? There is no vegetation on here. Nothing to burn or make a fire with.'

'But we can't stay here. There's no food, no water. No shelter. We'll die out here.'

'At last, the penny drops,' Liam grunted.

'We could swim for it. While we still have the strength.' Tyler said, desperately looking for a way out.

'Don't be stupid.' Liam snapped, clambering to his feet. 'Are you deaf? It's at least a hundred miles to land. Do you think you can do that? Swim a hundred miles? You wouldn't make it a mile. You know what's out there. What's waiting for us. You think it won't attack the second my dad gets in the water and it smells the blood from his leg wound?'

'We can't just stay here,' Tyler snapped, glaring at them both. And hoping that repeating it for the second time would make something change.

'If you think of anything, feel free to let us know. It's not like we want this or knew what would happen.'

Tyler stared out at the water and listened to the waves lap against the rocks. It was just after dawn, and already hot. The day was going to be punishing to them with no protection from the sun. He stood and stretched, then headed away from them.

'Where are you going?' Nash said.

'Checking this place out. There might be something you

missed.

'Trust me, there's nothing to see,' Liam said.

'My days of trusting you are long gone,' Tyler said as he walked away from them, intent on exploring the island.

II

The terms exploring and island both proved to be optimistic descriptions as the rock pile they were stranded on was too small to be able to do the former or be called the latter. It was essentially a large single rock jutting out of the ocean. A short 'beach' of smaller rocks and boulders was where Nash and Liam waited and watched him explore. The bulk of the rock was around fifteen feet tall and had become pitted and worn with exposure to the elements. Tyler looked at it and it was definitely scalable. For now, he dismissed it, instead picking his way around the edge, careful not to twist his ankle on the smaller loose rocks at his feet. The tide washed in, soaking his feet and ankles. It was only then he realised that he was both barefoot and still wearing his wetsuit. He picked his way around the giant rock, trying to ignore the lack of vegetation. The rear of the island was much the same as the front. A small depression had been partially eroded into the rock face, but not deep enough to provide them with any shelter from the elements. He stepped into it, checking anyway as the tide smashed against the rocks at his back. The depression in the rock was only two feet deep and seven high, and completely open to the elements. With some building materials, they might have been able to make a shelter. He chuckled a sharp bark that echoed from the rock at the idiocy of the thought. Building materials. Or a boat. Or a lifeguard. May as well wish for any of those things as they were just as unlikely. He ran his hand across the cool rock, hoping to find fresh water and seeing instead just a covering of moss creeping up the lower part of the wall. As desperate as the situation was, he wasn't quite prepared to eat *that* yet, and so he moved on around the back of the island so that he was on the opposite side to where Nash and Liam waited. It was cooler here with the sun rising on the north side and not yet warming the stone. He stared at the upper portion of the rock face. This route looked easier to climb, but the penalty for falling was higher. Sharp boulders jutted like deadly daggers to await anyone who may lose a foothold or slip on the slick rocks. At best, it would be a broken ankle or severe laceration. At worse, death. He reached up and grabbed a jutting section of rock, pulling himself up onto his tiptoes, testing his strength. How long, he wondered, would that last with no food or water and exposed to the burning heat of the day? It was then he knew that there was no other option. He would climb whilst he still could, otherwise, he knew it would nag at him that he hadn't explored every option. There was, however, a flaw in his plan. He looked down at his feet, his bare, wet feet and knew attempting to climb was madness. Nash had shoes on, or one at least, and as much as he didn't particular want to wear someone else's footwear, he decided he would ask to borrow them when he returned to the front of the island. He carried on, every step confirming what he had been told. There was nothing there. Just rock and crashing waves. He came back around the other side of the island, passing Liam on his way.

'Seen for yourself now?'

Tyler glared at him. 'You don't have to be a dick all the time. We're in this together.'

'You do what you want, man. I'd have saved my energy if I were you. You're gonna need it.'

'We all are. Don't talk to me like this is my fault. This was your show, not mine.'

'You don't know how lucky you were back there. You should be dead now.'

'That's enough, Liam,' Nash said, glaring at his son. 'Bickering isn't going to help anyone. We need to figure out a plan.'

Tyler turned to Nash, the anger threatening to boil over. 'You have something in mind?'

Nah frowned, one good eye refusing to focus on Tyler. 'No, but…it doesn't mean we shouldn't try. You really don't remember what happened, do you?'

'I told you. I remember hitting the water when the shark hit the boat. Everything else after is a blur.'

'It might come back to you. Just your brain flipping the circuit breakers and maybe threw a short circuit. It's been a tough time.'

Tyler offered no reply and looked out again at the undulating ocean. 'What the hell are we going to do?'

The lack of answer worried Tyler, although it didn't surprise him. It wasn't just that their options were limited; they were non-existent. He turned to Nash, watching as he touched the edges of his leg wound.

'We can't just wait here to die. We have to try something. You guys know the area and these waters. We need some options.'

'You know as much as we do. You also know what is in these waters. We can't go in there.'

'We can't stay here either. With this heat and no shade, we'll be dead within a couple of days.'

'That's not even the worst part. Without water, we're fucked,' Liam said, still defiant, still trying to be the big man. Tyler didn't want to get into another shouting match, and so he turned away and stared at the ocean. As he watched, the immense fin resurfaced. It made its way from right to left, slow and calculating around forty feet offshore.

'It's back. The shark. Are you seeing this?' Tyler said, turning to look at the other. However, neither Nash nor Liam seemed surprised.

'We know,' Nash said. 'He's stalking the edge of the shallows. It knows we're here.'

'Sharks don't do that. They don't do grudges.'

'This isn't a grudge. We're in its territory. Every twenty minutes or so, he'll swim on by just to remind us he's still there.'

Tyler watched as the fin sank beneath the waves. 'It can't come any closer?'

'No. The water here is too shallow for him. We're safe enough.'

'Trapped more like,' Liam said.

Tyler sat down hard, staring at the ocean. Everything that had happened was finally starting to sink in and the gravity of their situation was becoming more and more apparent to him with every passing moment.

NIGHT

Despite the intense, burning heat of the day, the night brought with it cold as the sea breeze assaulted their island. With no protection from the elements, they each tried as best they could to conserve their energy. The south side of the rock, where Tyler had found the hollow, was being relentlessly smashed by waves which made sleep difficult. Nash struggled, too, moaning in pain as his leg continued to weep blood as he drifted in and out of sleep. All day, the shark had continued to sweep past their island prison, making them aware of its presence. Tyler was glad for the dark just because he couldn't see the dorsal fin sweeping passed, first right to left, then the other way. He lay on his side, curled against the rock face, knees pulled up to try and keep warm. He drifted in and out of sleep, on the edge of consciousness. Memories drifted in and out of his mind as he ignored the hunger and thirst that was already starting to become a problem. He thought of his childhood, long-forgotten snippets of memories that were completely meaningless. He remembered playing in the street with childhood friends when the worries of adulthood were so far away. He remembered excited gift opening on Christmas morning, the security of the family unit around him bringing his troubled mind some comfort. He also dreamed of drink. Precious alcohol. Now the shock had subsided, and the monster in the water was no longer a threat, the other monster, the one that lived inside him, was raging and desperate to be fed. Telling himself there was nothing he could to about it was no help. It still thrashed and raged, demanding alcohol.

Across the island from Nash and Tyler as they struggled to sleep, Liam sat on a rock staring at them. There would be no sleep for him. Not under the circumstances. He sat and stared at his father and the stranger they had brought with them and considered the possibility that in order to survive, he may have to go to extreme lengths. There was no loyalty. No family, not now. It had become a battle for survival. Liam stared at the two other men and listened to the sound of the waves crashing against the rock. He was still there when the sun started to rise.

DAY 2

Tyler snapped awake. The dream had been vivid and frightening, and for a moment he lay there and let his heart slow to something akin to normal. It was early, and the sun had only just started to touch the rock that was their new home. The heat on his back was already intense and he knew the day ahead was going to be a long one. His throat was dry, and he opened and closed his mouth to try without success to generate some saliva. The dreams that had plagued him through the night had intensified, the worst of which was about the dive. He had replayed it in horrific detail in his mind as the giant shark had appeared out of the dark and changed their lives forever. Something about the dream had troubled him. There was an aspect to it which didn't fit or seem right yet he still couldn't place what it was. He sat up, squinting at the sun. It was a glorious morning the sky pale and cloudless. It would have been beautiful if it wasn't for the dire circumstances. Liam was sitting on a rock, staring at him.

'How long have you been awake?' Tyler asked.

'Not slept.' The answer was robotic and without emotion.

'Oh,' Tyler replied, rubbing his shoulder. It had gone numb where he had been sleeping on it. He turned to Nash, who was also awake and sitting upright, ravaged leg stretched out in front of him, the wound already attracting the attention of flies.

'You don't need to say it. I know it's bad.'

Tyler looked away. 'It will be fine. We'll get help.'

'Do you have a plan?' Nash replied, his voice full of hope.

Tyler shook his head. 'No, no I was just saying. We'll be fine.' He turned his attention to the ocean and the spot where their boat had been. 'Maybe it's moved off now. I still think we can try to get out of here.'

'He's gone nowhere.' Nash replied, wincing as he shifted position. 'This is his territory. His place. We're trapped.'

'You don't know that. You can't know that. Maybe it realised it couldn't get to us and moved off to feed elsewhere.'

'Then why not swim for it? See what happens,' Liam said. Despite everything that had happened to them, the arrogance was still there and was growing.

'Maybe I will. We'll die if we stay. At least that way we'll have a chance.'

'"We?" No, not we. You. We're staying here,' Liam snapped.

'For what? You said so yourself, there isn't any help coming. For whatever reason, we're stuck here. I don't know if you noticed, but that leg injury of your fathers is serious and not getting any better. We can't just stay here.'

'Then go. Swim for it. We'll watch and see how far you get before you either drown or get eaten by that fucking shark.'

'Enough both of you,' Nash shouted. He was staring at them both, his face slick with sweat. 'Stop bickering. This shouldn't have gone down this way, we know that. All we can do is deal with what we have. We've got no food, no water, and no way off this rock. Maybe he's right, maybe the two of you should try it and leave me here.'

Liam sighed and stood. He had tied the wetsuit around his waist and took one of the arms and wiped the sweat from his forehead. 'I won't leave you here to die alone.'

Tyler was only half-listening. Something had caught his eye in the water off the island, although he couldn't tell if it was a trick of the light. Whatever it was out there was only thirty feet out. Easily swimmable under ordinary circumstances. He turned to Nash. 'There's something out there in the water.'

Liam joined Tyler at the water's edge, cupping his face to shield it from the glare of the sun. 'Where?'

'Right there,' Tyler said, pointing to the spot off the coast.

'That's the Zodiac, or what's left of it. Junk.'

'What if we could use it? What if we could repair it? Wouldn't that give us at least half a chance?'

'Repair it with what? Besides, that looks pretty close to where the shark was stalking. Maybe too close,' Liam replied, still staring with his hands cupped.

'He's right,' Nash added. 'We're safe here because it's definitely too shallow. Out there, you're right on the edge. You won't be able to tell from the water if it's shallow or deep. Too risky.'

'I'm prepared to try it. We need to at least try,' Tyler said, driven more by the burning desire for a drink than any sense of bravery.

Liam glanced at his father, then at Tyler. 'I still say it's a risk. Are you feeling brave enough to try or are you just talking shit to look like the big man?'

Tyler had reached his breaking point. The desire to hit Liam was strong, and as frustration and exhaustion set in, he was finding it increasingly hard to hold it back. Without another word, Tyler turned back towards the water and waded in.

II

He had done it as a way of proving that he wasn't scared, but now that he was in the water and knew what was out there, he was much less confident. Even the little voice he thought of as his monster with it's never ending craving for booze was silent. He swam, forcing himself to be calm and not splash too much. He thought it was unlikely that the Megalodon was still stalking the island and waiting for them. A creature of such size would need to feed on more substantial meals than they would provide. He believed that, as he had said to the others, it had likely moved off after realising they were unobtainable prey. Even so, he couldn't escape the feeling of powerlessness and just how small he was. He risked a look back, and the island they were marooned on seemed even smaller. He focussed on the task at hand, swimming to the orange glow he could see just beneath the surface of the water and trying not to think about what could be below him. The Zodiac partially deflated, bobbing just beneath the surface and retaining enough buoyancy to keep it and the outboard engine from sinking. He tried not to get too excited at the idea that this could be their way out, but still felt a mini surge of adrenaline. He dived, kicking towards the part deflated boat and pulling it towards the surface. It was heavy, but the buoyancy helped. He resurfaced, gasping and treading water. Now there was no hiding his elation. This could be it. Their way back to the real world, their—

He was broken from his train of thought by something moving underneath him, the current caused by its wake pulling him a further ten feet away from the island. He stopped moving, partly through fear, partly through recollection of the book Nash had given him saying that kicking and splashing attracted sharks. He clutched his prize, determined not to let it go. There was something beneath the surface, an immense shape coming towards him.

Death.

It would find him first before the others and he could live with that. It was better than the alternative, the slow painful expiration that would come on the island if the Zodiac wasn't repairable. He flinched as the water exploded beside him and waited for the huge jaws of the creature to close around him and crush him. Once again, though, luck was with him. Instead of being crushed, Tyler was looking at a humpback whale. It had breached the surface, massive eye staring at him. Unlike his encounter with the shark, there was no sense of threat, just one of wonder at being in the presence of such a huge and graceful creature. Tyler was once again reminded that he was a minuscule part of the machine that was nature, one that would go on without him. He had read stories about whales helping humans. Even now, science was still learning about the incredible majesty and intelligence of the species. Tyler stared at it and wondered if this was some kind of sign that everything was going to be alright. He clutched the semi-inflated raft closer to him, treading water and wondering if the others could see what was going on. As he contemplated this, the whale lurched out of the water, emitting a high-pitched whine as it was attacked from below by the Megalodon. For a terrifying second, Tyler couldn't move and only watch the savage display as the whale was decimated. The wake from the attack pushed him back as the water bloomed with blood. It was this that spurred him on his way. He started to swim, desperately clinging on to the raft and listening to the sounds of the whale being savaged at his back. He made it back to the island, dragging the remains of the boat with him and wondering if it had all been worth it. Liam and Nash were waiting. All three of them were silent as the destruction continued, the cries of the whale and thrashing in the water an awful soundtrack to the devastation. When it was done, there was little evidence that any attack had taken place apart from a slick of blood on the surface of the water. Both Megalodon and remains of the whale were gone.

Tyler was still sitting at the water's edge, clinging to the remains of the inflatable. 'We're stuck here.'

'I told you we were,' Liam replied. 'No way we're leaving this place now. You just risked your life for nothing.'

III

The afternoon heat was unbearable. Nash was talking to Liam about trying to catch fish, although Tyler had noted there was little enthusiasm. There were no tools to make a net with. Tyler had made another lap of their small island, hoping to see something new he may have missed the first time around, yet there was no such luck. The rock was as barren as it had been the previous day and offered little in the way of provisions. This time, there was no second thought and he ate the moss without hesitation. Hunger and thirst had come much quicker than he ever anticipated. Even the monster that lived in him would settle for water now. It was as if the energy he had was being drained by the heat of the sun. Part of him wished he hadn't expended so much of his reserves retrieving the raft. Although potentially repairable, there was nothing to patch the hole in the rubber, and so it was useless. His lips were starting to become cracked and his tongue felt shrivelled in his mouth. When he returned to the front of the island, Liam was cleaning his father leg wound. He glanced at Tyler, the look in his eye saying that the prognosis was not good. The discolouration was increasing rapidly and infection had definitely set in.

'Bad, isn't it?' Nash said. Both Liam and Tyler were surprised how jovial he was considering the situation.

'Yeah, it's not looking too good, Dad,' Liam said, covering the wound with the makeshift bandage made from part of his wetsuit. 'We need to keep it clean.'

Nash chuckled and shifted position. 'I wouldn't worry about it. We'll be gone long before infection sets in. Couple more days and…well, that's us.'

'You don't know that.'

'I know enough. This isn't how it was meant to go down, that's for sure.'

An image flashed into Tyler's mind of the dive and the attack by the shark. It was as if the missing link in his memory had been found, and everything fit together exactly how he knew it should. 'Just how was it supposed to go down?' he said, glaring at Nash.

The older man stammered and looked away. 'I just mean we were unlucky.'

'No. That's not it. I remember when I was down there. How those drones of yours that were supposed to give us light. They moved towards the shark when it approached. As if someone were guiding them.'

'You're confused, it's just your brain playing tricks, that's all.'

'No, for the first time it's clear. You moved them towards the shark, didn't you?' Tyler recalled what happened the way the drones had exploded. At first, he thought it was because the shark had attacked them, but now as he replayed it in his mind, he knew that wasn't the case. 'You put explosives in the drones, didn't you?'

'I don't know what you're talking about,' Nash grunted.

'Hey, leave him alone, what the hell is wrong with you?' Liam stepped between his father and Tyler, but there was no stopping him now. He needed to say it.

'You used us as bait. You knew that thing was down there and would come for us. It was never about gold, was it? It was about revenge for what happened to you all those years ago.'

'Shut up, just shut up. It's not true.' Nash was flustered and agitated.

'It all makes sense. What was supposed to happen? We go down there to draw it out, you send your explosives-filled drones to kill it and get your revenge for what it did to you then we rake up the treasure at the end? Or were we supposed to die down there, too, leaving it all for you?'

'You're not making sense, the sun is making you crazy,' Nash screamed.

'Why don't you just admit it? The plan you had failed and now we're all stuck here. You fucking killed us.'

'I'm not admitting anything. You've got sunstroke or something. Don't you try to put this on me.'

'You heard him. Leave him alone,' Liam said, glaring at Tyler. The anger was still surging through him, but he knew well enough that getting into a fight would expend more energy than there was to waste. Instead, he went to the place he now referred to as his on the rock and dragged the deflated raft with him; he had, after all, earned it and so it was his. Not wanting anything more to do with Liam or his father, Tyler pulled the raft over his head, giving him a little respite from the sun. As he lay there on the hot rocks with anger surging through him, he was more determined than ever to get off the island and to freedom, even if it meant doing so at the expense of Nash and Liam.

IV

Night.

Without the burning heat of the sun and the alarming hunger and thirst, it could almost be paradise. Countless stars were painted across the sky which was cloudless and crisp. Tyler lay on the deflated raft, one end rolled into a pillow of sorts. He was on his back, staring at the sky and wondering if life out there was as cruel and brutal as it was on earth. He hadn't spoken to the others since the argument earlier, and even though his anger had cooled, he was just as certain that everything he had accused Nash of was true, even if there was no way to prove it. He tried to clear his throat, but it was too dry. He would have given anything for a glass of water, just to clear away that dryness.

'Hey.'

Tyler looked to his right. Nash was staring at him in the gloom of the moonlight. Beyond him, Liam was on his side, sleeping.

'I've got nothing else to say to you.'

'Then just listen,' Nash said, his voice a near whisper barely audible above the crashing waves. 'You were right.'

'About what?'

'Everything. I wanted it dead. That bastard thing ruined my life.'

Tyler turned to face him. 'So why deny it? Why the denial earlier?'

'I can't let my son know. Just believe me when I tell you that neither of you was supposed to be in the firing line for this. You were supposed to stay still on the bottom. The explosives in the drones were supposed to kill the shark from safely above you. Remember I told you? I said stay on the bottom. If you had just done what I said, it would have worked.'

'It was a crazy plan,' Tyler hissed, too tired to get angry.

'It could have worked. Even if the explosives didn't kill it, then it would have scared the shark away, hopefully; left it disfigured like me.'

'Unbelievable.'

'I don't expect you to understand. I just wanted to set the record straight,' Nash grunted.

'No, I understand perfectly. Your lifetime vendetta against this monster came down to revenge. When it went wrong, it put us all in danger to the point where it's going to cost us all our lives. But at least you have a clear conscience, right?'

Nash frowned and looked out over the black waters. 'It was about revenge. No point in denying that. But my conscience ain't clear. Not by a long shot.'

'Then why say anything? What does it achieve? Why not just keep quiet.'

'Because we don't have long left. Another day or so and we're done for. We can't survive like this. At least now it's all out on the table.'

Tyler nodded past Nash to Liam. 'What about him? Doesn't he deserve the truth?'

Nash glanced at his then back to Tyler. 'He wouldn't handle it. He's not calm like you. He gets…angry. Volatile. He has medication for his brain, but of course, it was lost on the boat. For him, it's best he thinks this was all an accident. It's important to keep him calm.'

'And what if I decide to tell him otherwise?'

Nash shrugged. 'I'll deny it. A son will always believe his father over a stranger. Besides, soon enough, it won't matter. Don't tell me you haven't felt it. The gnawing in your belly, the delirium, the need for water.'

Tyler said nothing. There was no need.

'Thing is,' Nash went on, 'is that human nature will take over. Soon enough, when desperation takes over, we'll see what the two of you are made of.'

'What do you mean?'

Nash smiled, the expression ghastly in the poor light. 'You know what I mean. When a man becomes desperate, all the rules go out of the window. It comes down to who wants to live the most and how far you are willing to go to do it.'

Despite the heat that was still embedded in the rocks, a chill surged through Tyler. 'You mention the two of us. Why not yourself?'

Nash chuckled. 'Isn't it obvious? I'm the weak link. Old and crippled. I'll be the first to die here, there's no doubt about that.'

'Nobody has to die here, Nash. There might be a way.'

'Only…there isn't. This isn't some bullshit novel or Hollywood movie. There isn't some third arc plot twist to get us out of the shit. The end is coming for us all; it's just a matter of how long it takes.'

'I won't give in. I won't just stay here and wait to die. You might and that's up to you, but not me.'

Nash shrugged. 'No, I don't think you will. I wonder which of you will do whatever it takes to live a little longer?'

'You sound sorry you won't get to see it.'

'I am. Both sorry and curious. I think you stand a good chance of survival all told. I just don't think you'll go as far as Liam will. That will be your downfall.'

'Yeah, well, I don't intend for it to come to that. I intend to do everything we can to make sure we live a little longer, *together*. There is always a chance.'

'Not always. Not now.'

Tyler turned on his side and pulled the deflated raft over him like a blanket. 'We better get some sleep. Save our energy.'

'You do that,' Nash said, staring out into the dark. 'You get your rest and save your energy.'

Tyler ignored him, and despite what he said, he knew that sleep would not come easily that night. On the opposite side of the rock, Liam lay with his eyes open, having listened to everything that had been said. He stared out to sea and imagined the waves were whispering to him and telling him what he had to do.

DAY THREE

The hunger and thirst woke Tyler before dawn. His body felt as if it had shrivelled, and he was wasting away hour by hour. To his surprise, when he woke, Liam was in the water. He was standing there up to his waist. Tyler could see ghostly shadows where his ribs were showing through his skin. Tyler sat beside Nash. 'What is he doing?'

'Fishing. He's had this crazy idea he saw on a film once to just stand there and be still until a fish comes close then he says he'll snatch it out of the water.'

Tyler glanced at Nash then watched Liam. 'Is that possible? It seems unlikely.'

'I told him that already. He won't listen to me. He does crazy stuff like this when he's off his meds.'

'He'll burn out there in this heat.'

'He's stubborn. Best to let him do it. I'm too tired to argue with him again. Like I said, he won't be all that rational now.'

It was the first time Tyler had realised how old and tired Nash looked. He seemed to have aged impossibly in a short space of time. He decided it was as good a time as any to try to talk to him about what happened during the dive without Liam's short fuse threatening to explode at any given moment. 'I want to talk to you about the dive,' he said, unsure how things would play out. To his surprise, Nash only sighed and wiped the sweat from his brow.

'My throat is so dry I don't know how much talking I have in me. Still, I suppose I owe you an explanation. After all, you were nothing to do with this. Wrong place wrong time.'

The nonchalant way he said it made Tyler angry, but he wanted answers and pushed his frustration aside. He waited, staring at his long, skinny shadow on the rocks in front of him.

'You have to understand,' Nash said, looking straight out to sea, his scars visible in horrific clarity. 'That thing ruined my life. I wish it had killed me.'

'No, you don't. You wouldn't have fought on for all these years dealing with those injuries if you thought that.'

'It's because of the way I look that I wish I was dead. You don't get it. You weren't there. It's bad enough dealing with how I look. It's the memories. People I knew, my brothers who were taken by that fucking thing. It savaged them. Every time I see this…mess that's left of me, it reminds me of them. It's like an open wound that can never heal. In some ways, I've never been away from the day I first saw it.

'Why now? Why wait until now to get your revenge if that's what this was all about?'

'Because I wasn't sure.' Nash glanced at Tyler then immediately looked away. 'Not until I heard about that gold being found. I suspected, of course, I did. Why do you think I chose to come and live out here? I was waiting for a chance to get my revenge. I just needed help.'

'And you chose me,' Tyler said.

Nash shook his head. 'Don't make it sound bad. You wanted the gold, I get that. Nobody forced you to do this. We gave you the opportunity.'

'No. You can't try to sell that story, Nash. You sold this as a simple dive to get some gold.'

'I told you the stories. The legend. I told you what was out here. Just because you chose not to believe it, that's not my fault.'

'Fine, that I'll give you. Using me as bait, that's on you, though. You can't talk your way out of that.'

'No, no I can't.'

They fell silent and watched Liam standing motionless in the water.

'For what it's worth, I'm sorry. Like I said, this wasn't how it was supposed to be. The drone was supposed to detonate when he bit into it and kill him. I never imagined…Well, you know.'

'Yeah, I know,' Tyler said, leaning his head back on the rocks and wishing for water. He didn't want booze anymore, though.

That was one relief. It seemed a slow agonising death was a fantastic cure for near alcoholism.

Twenty feet away, Liam stood in the shallows and stared at the shimmering ocean. He had detached himself from the world. The fear, the hunger. The thirst. All of it now felt as if it belonged to somebody else. The water lapped against his abdomen, the sounds of the water like voices telling him what he needed to do. He wasn't religious by any mean, but now was silently praying to the god he hoped existed. Not only for a way out but also for the strength to do what he knew was necessary. The brutal, inhuman things he would be forced to undertake to ensure he lived. He had asked his questions and was still waiting for an answer yet to arrive. He was starting to consider that his lack of answer was enough of an answer to his query when something touched his cheek. He blinked and turned his eyes to the sky. This time, there was no mistake.

Rain.

Water.

The strength he had asked for and also the go ahead with the barbaric and brutal things he was going to have to do. The rain started to fall faster, pattering the ocean around him. He opened his mouth and let it land on his parched tongue.

Water. The biggest problem, the biggest drain on his strength was now given to him. As he heard his father and Tyler cheer and whoop as the rain fell, he didn't smile or change his expression. The strength to do his job was now on its way. He just needed to find the will to do it.

CHAPTER NINE

The rain was ferocious, driven from the heavens with a fury unlike anything any of them had ever seen. They whooped and cheered, revelling in the unexpected lifeline. Tyler had made the inflatable into a container to collect the precious water and was holding it in place to stop it blowing off the rock. Nash and Liam had their faces turned to the sky, mouths open as they took in the precious life-giving water. Such a simple thing as rainfall had given renewed hope and energy after the punishment of the previous days. With the joy of receiving the precious water came also fear, as the tiny rock they were stranded on was pounded by waves churned up by the storm. They watched the storm rage above them, sky alive with lightning, the power of nature in evidence all around them it was both exhilarating and terrifying at the same time.

Later, when the storm passed, they sat in contemplation.

'That should buy us a few days,' Nash said, looking from Liam to Tyler. 'Now all we need is for it to rain food and we'll be set.'

'I was actually thinking about that,' Liam said, shuffling closer to the others.

'You've had an idea?' Tyler said.

'Not an idea as such, a suggestion.'

'Go on.'

He glanced out to the black ocean, then at the others, his face milky in the moonlight. 'I was thinking about you, Dad; more specifically, your leg. You know, how infected it is.'

'Yeah, it's not looking too good, is it?' Nash said, staring at the discoloured appendage.

'You need help, at a hospital, even then I think we all know the odds are you'll lose it. That kind of infection isn't easy to come back from.'

'You're killing my good mood here, son.'

Liam shifted position again, and now addressed Tyler directly. It was the first time he had seemed civil and without the chip on his shoulder.

'We could help him. Cut it off, the leg. Stop the infection from spreading. If we catch it quickly, we might be able to save it above the knee.'

'Are you insane? That's not an option. It's not possible. Tell him, Nash.'

Nash looked from his leg to his son, and Tyler could see it. The older man was afraid. He wondered if that had always been the case, that he feared his son and he had never noticed it before. Liam went on.

'Think about it, we need food. We could take off the leg, save dad's life and then…then we'll have something to eat as long as we avoid the infected areas.'

Silence.

Nobody wanted to speak or knew what to say. The waves lapped at their rock prison and still, nobody broke the silence brought on by Liam's words. Tyler cleared his throat, choosing his words carefully.

'We're all hungry, I get that. But this line of thought leads nowhere. This isn't an option. Granted, the leg wound is infected, but we don't know if the infection will spread or not. It could be isolated and saveable once we get out of here. Even if we needed to take the leg, if it was a life-threatening injury that meant it had to happen, we have no way of doing it. No tools, nothing to stop the bleeding, nothing to numb his pain. No means of stitching or sealing the wound. He wouldn't survive. Even if by some miracle he did, the risk of infection would be even bigger with a fully open wound. And for what? A hunk of infected meat that you couldn't cook or make safe to eat. It's a non-starter.' Even as he said it, Tyler tried to rid his mind of images of rare steak served with peppercorn sauce. Disgusted by the way his mind made the link, he swallowed the burst of saliva before he could start to drool.

He looked to Nash for support, but he was still staring at his son, a frail and frightened old man.

'Take it easy,' Liam said, breaking eye contact. 'It was just…I wasn't thinking. I'm so hungry, so so hungry it's just…' He stared at his father's leg, then forced himself to look away. 'I wasn't thinking straight, that's all. I get like this when I'm off my medication.'

'I get it, but I'm telling you right here and now. Get that idea out of your head. We have water now and can ration it out which means we've bought a little time. We'll figure out a way to get food. We're surrounded by ocean that is full of life. We'll figure out a way to get it.'

'Yeah, you're right, forget I mentioned it. I'm just…I don't know. I'm not quite together anymore. This place is breaking me.'

They had all felt it but Nash was first to vocalise it.

'You know, maybe it might be better to just end this. Just walk out into the sea and let that bastard finish us.' Nash wouldn't look at them as he said it. Instead, he stared out over the ocean with his one good eye. The shark had stopped patrolling the island, but they all knew it was out there.

'We can't give up. Not now. Look at how bad things were before we got water,' Tyler said, not liking the dark thread they were following.

'With no food, it will get worse. I don't know about you, but I'm feeling weaker every day. To just sit here and die…It won't be a good way to go.'

'Look, I think we're all feeling negative tonight. Let's get some rest and save our strength. We'll talk tomorrow.'

Nobody had the energy to argue. Nash settled down and made himself as comfortable as he could. Tyler did the same, his exhausted mind and body meaning sleep came easier than it should have.

Liam, however, didn't sleep. He sat there in the dark and stared at his father's leg. He started to drool.

PRE-DAWN

Nash and Tyler were still sleeping. Liam was too agitated and hungry to do the same and wanting to remove himself from them both, especially his father's leg and the chance to survive it would have presented, he had gone to the other side of their tiny island, just so he could be alone with his thoughts. The hunger burned in his gut, which he was sure had shrivelled to something non-existent. Hungry eyes scanned the surface of the rock island, looking for something, anything to eat. He found the debris in the alcove. He presumed the storm had pushed it to the island. Liam crouched in the alcove, sifting through the floating fragments of fibreglass. There was half a soggy paperback, it's cover missing. Alongside it was a few little pieces of polystyrene and half a plastic mug that was his fathers and was cracked down one side. He ignored all of it. The thing that caught his eye was the box. Designed to be positively buoyant in the event of falling overboard, he knew it was the sign from above he had been waiting for. He pulled it towards him, shaking hands fumbling with the catch. Eventually, he freed it and lifted the lid. Inside the watertight container was a medical kit. Liam pushed past the bandages and found what he was looking for at the bottom. He took out the scalpel, heart thundering. There were also spare blades in the box and flare gun. In that instant, everything changed. The opportunity that had, until that point, not allowed him to follow his initial train of thought was now there. Something wet touched his leg, and for a moment, he thought it was starting to rain. It was only when he looked at it that he realised he was drooling at the idea of finally getting some food. Now all he needed was the mental strength to do what he had to so they could survive. He rolled his sunken eyes to the sky. 'Please, show me a way to do this. Show me a way to make it happen.'

He waited and listened to the water crash against the rocks, hoping for some kind of message from above. He was aware that the sun was starting to rise, and that he should get back before the others woke and found him missing. First, though, he would need to hide his new find.

When he had finished hiding the box under some loose rocks in the alcove and returned to the front of the island, the day was already starting to heat up. He arrived back at their makeshift campsite and found Tyler crouched beside Nash. At first, he thought they were just in conversation until he saw his father's unblinking gaze staring at the sky.

'It must have happened overnight,' Tyler said. 'It looks like he just slipped away.'

Liam approached, staring at his father, unsure why he didn't feel anything. Tyler didn't know what to say. Death made him uncomfortable at the best of times, but here on the hot, tiny island prison that had become their home, it was even worse. He had always held out hope that they would be saved and escape, but now as he looked at the empty vessel sprawled on the sand, the reality of the situation had shattered the fragile illusion he had built and with it reduced the symphony of questions in his mind down to just one.

How will we survive?

It was a good question. Hope was no longer enough. He looked across to Liam, wishing there were words he could say that would make a difference. He knew there were none. Liam, for his part, seemed to be taking the death of his father well. He was kneeling by the body, brow dotted with sweat, sunken eyes taking in the sight and trying to make sense of it.

'Are you okay?' Tyler asked, the simple function of speech becoming harder as his energy faded.

Liam had no answer. He simply stared, brow furrowed, sweat collecting on the tip of his nose.

'Liam?'

'How long has he been dead?'

There was no emotion in his voice. It was flat and almost disinterested.

'I don't know. I woke up and thought he was still sleeping. It wasn't until the sun shone on his face and he didn't move that I realised...'

Liam nodded, satisfied with the explanation. 'You know this changes things for us, don't you?' He looked at Tyler, dark and bottomless.

Despite the heat, Tyler felt a flush of cold. 'Changes things how?'

'My dad is dead, but it doesn't mean we have to go the same way. We have a chance now without him.'

'Maybe now isn't the time. We can talk about it later. You need time to mourn, to get to grips with what has happened.' Tyler was shaken by the dismissiveness Liam was showing. There was no sorrow or mourning for his father. He wondered if it was nothing more than survival instinct kicking in or if the heat, thirst, and hunger had simply combined to throw a few switches into the off position in his brain. Tyler couldn't really argue the point, though. His first thought after discovering Nash was dead had been that they might now be able to risk heading out into open water without worrying about Nash bleeding into it and drawing in the Megalodon. Despite what he had just said, he understood now was the time to act if they intended to try and escape the island. Every wasted second brought them closer to death.

'Did you have something in mind? To get us off this rock, I mean. '

Liam looked out over the water, rocking on his haunches. 'No. Not for that. Not yet. We're too weak for that now.'

'You just said you thought we had a chance.'

'We do.' Liam looked at him then, half his face cast in gold by the sun. 'Way I see it, we need to get our strength before we try to escape. To do that, we need energy. That means food.'

There was nothing more he needed to say. A quick flick of the eyes towards his dead father said more than any words could. Tyler felt the shriveled up thing that was now his stomach tighten even more.

'You can't be serious. We've discussed this. We're not that desperate. Not yet. '

'I think we are. I'm not the only one who feels it.'

'Feels what?'

'The strength and energy ebb away by the hour. How long do you think we can go on like this? A day? A week? We need to do something now before it's too late if we intend to get off this island and passed that shark.'

'I can't do that. I won't do that. You're talking about

cannibalism.'

Liam shook his head. 'No. I'm talking about survival. It's different.'

'That's your father, not a slab of meat. Jesus, can you hear yourself?'

'You don't know him. This is what he would have wanted. He'd want us to live.'

'He didn't seem too sure on the idea when you first brought it up. If I remember, he looked as disgusted as I feel.'

'He'd understand,' Liam snapped. He was twitching and looked almost animalistic as he crouched there. 'Besides, I'm not asking for your permission.'

'I can't stop you. Just don't expect me to do it. Are things really so desperate you feel this is the only option? We're not in that place yet where we need to do this.'

Liam laughed, a sharp sound that had no place in such a desolate place under such horrific circumstances. 'You think I don't know that? You think I want to do this? I don't have a choice.'

'There's always a choice. Look, I know you and I haven't gotten along during this trip. But your father asked me to come, and I'd like to think as the elder man here, you might listen to me when I tell you this isn't something you want to do. It's a mistake. It's something you will have to live with for the rest of your life if you do it. Your father told me about your medication, and how not having it can make you think differently.'

'What the hell do you know about it? It's not your business. You don't know anything about me.'

'I know I want to help you. We need to stick together if we want to get out of here. The odds are already stacked against us.'

'You say it like there is another choice. You think I want to do this?'

'Then don't. We'll figure out a different way. This isn't something you want to have to live with if you do it.'

Liam shook his head. 'We'll die if I don't. It won't matter either way.'

'But what if we live? What if we figure this out or someone rescues us? What then? How will you handle it back home when it's all you can think about? All you can…Taste. It will haunt you forever.' Tyler knew well enough about need. His booze addiction which had been repressed by the need to survive, had been revived by the rain, and once it had tasted water, it now wanted something a little stronger and was thrashing around his gut again. He composed himself and continued. 'I'm just trying to save you from that kind of trauma. I'm trying to help you here. '

Liam stared at him, then looked at his father. 'I don't know what I'm saying anymore. My mind seems like it belongs to someone else.'

Tyler shuffled closer, trying to ignore the fear, the heat and the thirst. Most of all, he was trying to ignore the images of steak, rare and bloody, that were flashing up in his mind. 'I can help you. We can help each other. This isn't the end. We still might have a chance to get off this island. If you do this, if you…if you do what you were talking about, then it's over. You'll have crossed a line you can never come back from.'

'I *don't* want this. That's the part you don't seem to understand. You keep looking at me like I'm a monster. I just…I'm so hungry. You must be, too.'

'Of course I am. But this isn't the answer. Please just think about it. Take some time.'

'What else do we have but time,' Liam muttered. Tyler had heard that before. He thought it might have been a quote from a

TV show, perhaps an old episode of The Twilight Zone, but he couldn't be sure.

'Exactly. No rush to take action yet. We have all the time in the world. You've just lost your father. With the shock and the weakness...It's no surprise things seem a little off. Please, just don't rush into anything you'll regret.'

'I think you're right. I need to take some time to think.'

'Good. You do that. Take some time.'

Tyler watched as Liam stood and walked out of sight around the back of their rock prison. It was only then he could relax. He leaned against the hot stone and stared at the body of Nash. For him at least, it was over. Tyler thought maybe he was the lucky one.

CHAPTER TEN

Time enough at last.

That had been the episode of The Twilight Zone he couldn't recall. He remembered it featured Burgess Meredith as the last man on earth after some kind of apocalyptic event. All poor Burgess had wanted was to be left alone to read in peace, something granted to him by said apocalypse and something he was happy about until the ultimate twist in the story resulting in the character played by Burgess breaking his reading glasses. With no optician available, the bittersweet irony dawned on him and left the viewer with a sour note as they wondered how poor Burgess would survive in the devastation without his ability to read (or see). Tyler was so set on remembering every aspect of the episode if only because it took his mind off the problem at hand.

His initial thought had been to float Nash's body out to sea, in doing so removing temptation from Liam and stopping him from making a savage and life changing decision. The first reason he decided against it was the Megalodon. He didn't want to bait the water and remind it that they were there. Although it had been a couple of days since they last saw it's fin slicing through the waters on the edge of the shallows, he suspected it was still out there, just waiting to see if they would venture back into its territory. The other reason, and one that was much more disturbing as to why he was unable to go through with it, was the sick idea that Liam was right and their only chance of survival was to eat some of Nash's remains. The idea terrified him but still didn't rid his mind of those images of steak and mushrooms cut with thick cut fries on the side. An explosion of saliva filled his mouth and he swallowed it, with some effort, back down.

He couldn't. He wouldn't. He…

Did Burgess own a bookstore?

Was that part of the irony of the long ago watched Twilight Zone episode?

He couldn't have been too old when he saw it. Maybe early teens. Why did it stick in his mind? Perhaps because he, too, was stuck and alone in a world that for all intents and purposes was empty. Nash was the equivalent of the reading glasses, and Tyler couldn't decide if he should break them or make sure he took extra care of them.

Besides. He *was* hungry. Good sense went out of the window when it came down to survival. Could he bring himself to eat human flesh? To eat it raw? He didn't think so. He wasn't in that place yet mentally. But the idea was becoming less and less of a taboo with each passing moment. Maybe Liam was right. Maybe the rules that had always governed the world went out of the window when it came down to the basics of survival. He stared at Nash's body and was already struggling to identify it as a human. It was a shell, meat and bones. Flesh.

Stop it.

The voice in his head was one of reason and served its purpose in derailing his morbid train of thought. Either way, he knew he couldn't stand to look at Nash anymore. He retreated to the semi-inflated raft and cupped a double handful of water. It was running low and would soon be gone. Tyler leaned on the rock and closed his eyes, wishing he knew what to do for the best.

Later

Darkness had started to shroud their little slice of hell. Since leaving Tyler, Liam had been at the rear of the island in the alcove. The medical kit was in front of him, the scalpel clutched in a grubby hand. He stared at it, fascinated as it bent the light from the falling sun. He liked the way it warped and twisted, thinking it was similar to how he felt inside. He turned his senses inward, listening to his body and trying to decipher what it was trying to say to him. There was confusion in there. And fear. That, he had learned was the worst. It had eaten away at him, hour by hour, day by day until now it ruled him. He had come to understand that fear made people do things they wouldn't normally do, and mad them behave in irrational ways. He thought of his father, a man with whom he hadn't always seen eye to eye, and a relationship that was at times distant and filled with frustration. Even so, Liam had always loved him. He wondered why he didn't feel anything now he was dead. There was sadness, true. But it was a different kind of sadness, similar to the kind when you see a celebrity death flash up on the news. There was surprise, a little shock, but no outpouring of grief. No agonising sorrow.

There was just the hunger.

That was ever present, and something which now ruled his entire existence. Feeding the hunger, satisfying that gnawing in his gut as his withered body screamed for sustenance.

It's what he would have wanted. He'd want you to survive.

The voice in his head didn't really even sound like him anymore. It had taken on its own personality, its own life. His medication usually stopped him from hearing it. It was designed that way to block out those dark things that spoke to him. Now, though, with that particular block lifted, it was free to converse as much as it wanted. The scalpel, it told him, was the answer. The answer to all his problems.

'What if I can't do it? Cut him…eat him…he will be raw,' he whispered to himself.

You can do it. You'll force yourself to keep it down because that's what you need to do to survive.

'He's my father.'

No. he was your father. Now he's just meat. A juicy steak or a nice piece of bacon.

Liam started to cry, silent sobs that were masked by the waves crashing against the rocks.

He knew the voice was right. He knew he had to act and ensure he didn't die. Even if it meant doing something that was truly appalling. He started to inch his way back around the island to where his father was.

And what about Tyler? the devious inner voice asked.

'What about him?'

What if he tries to stop you?

It was a good question. He didn't think it would happen. He would be repulsed, that much was obvious, but he didn't think he would interfere.

And if he does?

Liam stopped, letting the water rush over his feet. 'If he does, I'll kill him.'

The voice said nothing, but Liam knew it was smiling wherever in his subconscious it lived.

When he got back to their camp, it was almost total dark. He could see Tyler snoozing by the yellow inflatable, head on his chest. Liam was pleased. It would be easier with him asleep and not aware of what was going on. He moved silently towards where his father's body still lay. In the glow of the moon, he looked like a shell, the shadows making him appear as a ghoul with black wells where his eyes should have been. Liam touched his father's head, the rough scar tissue cold to the touch.

'I hope you understand why I'm doing this,' he whispered as he brought the knife out. His hands were shaking and he had to focus to steady them. 'We have to live, we have to survive.'

With his free hand, he grabbed his father's cold wrist and straightened it, touching the point of the scalpel blade to the meaty part of the forearm. 'Forgive me.' Liam said, then he cut.

The blood looked black in the moonlight. Liam cut a strip of flesh from the forearm, the tears streaming freely down his face. His mind was filled with static, the horror of his actions too much to bear, too much for him to handle. He had slipped into autopilot as he cut the lump of flesh loose. He held it in his palm, lip trembling.

'What's going on, what are you doing?' Tyler said, sitting upright.

'Just stay back, this is nothing to do with you,' Liam said, the sobs getting heavier. He looked at the lump of flesh in his hand and knew what he had to do. His stomach churned and growled, then, in an event that repulsed him more than he ever anticipated, he started to drool. Thick strands of saliva hung from his chin as he looked at the grisly lump of flesh.

'Don't do it; you'll regret it if you do,' Tyler said, standing but not approaching. He had seen the scalpel shimmering in the moonlight and wondered dimly in the back of his mind where it had come from.

'This is my business. I'm so hungry,' Liam whined as the drool fell to the bloody rocks in front of him. 'You keep out of it.'

Tyler watched, too stunned to do anything else. Liam lifted the lump of flesh to his mouth, caught between desire and disgust, hunger and repulsion. He was balanced there on a knife edge, when that little voice so silent and sly, whispered in his mind and encouraged him to do it.

Knowing he could delay no longer for fear he would change his mind, he put it in his mouth and started to chew.

Pork gristle sprang to mind, chewy and tough, resistant to his efforts to eat it. He could taste blood, and feel the fine hairs on what was his father's arm tickling the inside of his mouth as he chewed on the cold, fleshy lump. He badly wanted to spit it out onto the rocks, but he couldn't do it. The voice in his head wouldn't let him. He chewed, trying to break up the fleshy lump as tears streamed down his beard-scruffed cheeks. He gagged, thought he was going to vomit, then gagged again but somehow kept control. The voice inside spoke up. Told him to keep chewing, to resist the urge to spit it out. Liam was breathing through his nose, rapid snorts as he came to terms with the decision he'd made. Somehow he managed to swallow, almost bringing it straight back up. He needed water, something to wash the vile taste from his mouth, and so he stood and stumbled towards Tyler, scalpel forgotten and still clutched in one bloody hand.

Misreading Liam's approach for water as some kind of attack with the scalpel, self-preservation took over and Tyler met the perceived attack. They grappled, Tyler holding the wrist of the hand holding the knife whilst at the same time trying to wrestle Liam to the ground, but the younger man was physically stronger, and with adrenaline surging as a result of what he had just done, was difficult to subdue. Liam, thinking Tyler had attacked without provocation, fought back, the voice in his mind telling him this was now a battle over food, and that Tyler wanted to take it from him. He unleashed a scream of rage and drove Tyler back, the older man losing his footing on the smooth rocks. Knowing he couldn't risk letting go of Liam and his knife arm, he clung on, both of them crashing to the ground. Tyler hit the edge of the inflatable, flipping it over and spilling the precious remaining water onto the rocks.

'The water, we lost the water,' Tyler said, trying to reason with Liam, but there was no way to make him listen. His eyes were wild, feral. He had stopped being a human and had taken on the traits of some kind of monster. Tyler realised how weak he was, and that the physical toll of their struggle was making him tire.

'What are you doing? Why are you attacking me?' he grunted, keeping his eye on the knife blade.

Liam blinked, and then a moment of clarity banished the voice and its commands back to where it lived. He understood then that a mistake had been made, a misunderstanding which had almost led to him trying to kill another human being. With such a sobering thought at the forefront of his mind, whatever had taken over him was gone. He rolled off towards the water, then scrambled back towards the body of Nash. Tyler sat up, breathing heavily as he looked at the overturned inflatable. 'That was all the water we had. What are we supposed to do now? What the hell did you attack me for?'

Liam stared at him, a skinny wretch, a blood-smeared shell of the healthy man who he had first met in the bar. 'I thought you wanted to take it from me,' he grunted.

'Take what?' Tyler said, even though he suspected he knew the answer.

The food. Liam was protecting his food.

'I was wrong. I understand that now. There is enough for us both,' Liam said, hopping back over his father's corpse and crouching again by the arm he had already cut a slice from. 'Try some. It's really not that bad. Look, I'll show you.'

Tyler stared, horrified and sickened as Liam cut another strip of flesh from his father's forearm. He held it up, showing it to Tyler by the light of the moon. 'Have you ever had sushi? It helps to just pretend that's what it is.' He slipped the sliver of flesh into his mouth, the wet sound of his chewing incredibly loud. He gagged once, then swallowed it down.

'What's happened to you?' Tyler said, not expecting a response.

'Don't you get it? We have to live. I'm not ready to die yet. This is the way it has to be.'

'Without water, we're fucked anyway. You realise that, right?'

Liam glared at him, then looked away. Tyler watched as he cut another slice of flesh off his father. This time, he didn't even flinch as he swallowed it. 'You'll see. You might have already given up, but I haven't. I'll survive this. I guarantee it.'

CHAPTER ELEVEN

The next day was explosively hot and Nash had started to spoil. His flesh was bloating and starting to crack, and every time the breeze rushed over the island, Tyler was hit with the sour rot smell. He hadn't slept, the combination of fear and his overactive brain making such a thing impossible to do. He had sat and watched as Liam had systematically eaten his father. By sunrise, the arm had been stripped down to the bone and Liam had moved on to the uninjured leg. As Tyler watched, he cut a slice of calf free and popped it into his mouth, resting one hand on his father's bloated stomach. The two men locked eyes across the rock beach.

'You sure you don't want some? It's starting to spoil,' Liam said between noisy chews.

Tyler couldn't help but notice how the terminology had changed. It seemed Liam no longer saw Nash as a person. Just food. Tyler would have said something, but he was too exhausted. He was sure he could feel his body wasting away and was almost envious of Liam who was rapidly regaining his vitality.

'You really should eat something,' Liam added. He grinned, his teeth bloody and covered with lumps of stringy flesh. 'Seriously, you'll feel better.'

'Where did you get the scalpel?' Tyler asked, the simple act of speaking taking a herculean effort.

Liam didn't answer at first. He simply chewed, hands and mouth caked in dried blood. 'Found a medkit from the boat washed up round the back of the island. Had all this stuff inside. Bandages. Antiseptic. The works. That's what I tried to explain, but you didn't understand.'

'There's nothing to understand.'

'I prayed for this. I asked for a sign, some proof that this was how it was meant to go down then boom. The kit washes up with everything I needed. I was going to ask Dad about the leg, to explain to him why it had to come off and that we had the equipment to make sure he survived. Only I was too late. At first, I was upset, but then it occurred to me.'

'What did?'

'That his death was a sign too. Some higher power.'

'You don't strike me as the religious type.'

'I'm not saying it was God. I'm not even sure if I believe in that stuff, but you have to admit it. *Something* has worked in our favour so far.'

Tyler laughed. He couldn't stop himself. It came out more as a series of dry coughs.

'What is it? What's so funny?'

'Worked in our favour? We are almost killed by a giant prehistoric shark, end up shipwrecked on a fucking rock with no food, you turn psycho and decide to eat your dead father, then to top it off, we lose all our fresh water. Oh yeah, someone is really looking out for us.'

'This is what we have to do to survive. There is no choice.'

Tyler struggled to his feet, feeling dizzy. 'And how do we do that? Swim for it? Call a taxi? How does what you're doing help us? Fucking look at it out there there's nothing...' He stopped speaking, sure he was hallucinating. There was a glimmer on the horizon, a white speck which he was certain wasn't there before. Forgetting all about Liam, he walked to the edge of the rock, cupping his eyes against the sun. He saw it again, a metallic glint on the horizon.

'Fuck, it's a boat, there's a damn boat out there!' Tyler

shrieked, not caring as adrenaline surged through him. He leapt and waved his arms, shouting even though it was unlikely they would be seen. 'Come on, help me signal for it,' he bellowed over his shoulder. Liam, however, just sat there and stared, looking from the horizon, to Tyler, then to the bloated remains of his father. His mind was filled with static, like a radio struggling to find a signal. Nothing made sense to him anymore nothing was rational or seemed ordinary. The life he once had, the life before, was gone. It seemed like something he could never get back even if they were rescued. That was when it reappeared, the monster inside, the voice free to speak as it chose without medication to dull it. It told him what was necessary, what the implications were if he didn't act. He knew in some distant, detached way that what he was being told was wrong, but also that things had already gone too far for him to ever recover from. He listened as the inner voice told him what he had to do and how to do it, and that the decision he was about to make was the best one under the circumstances. He tightened his grip on the scalpel, then lurched to his feet and tackled Tyler from behind, pitching him forward onto the hard rocks, his upper half landing in the water. Liam grabbed the back of Tyler's head and pushed it under the water, waiting for him to die. Just like the voice had told him to.

II

Captain Adam Carrington might have missed the call for help if not sailing upon the debris field. He and his three-man crew had been leaning overboard the hundred and twenty-foot vessel, visually scanning the floating debris for anything that may be salvageable. His men knew of the legends of the area about the monster shark which supposedly roamed the waters, and to see the floating debris field had initially spooked them. It was only by chance as Carrington was scanning the landscape with his binoculars that he saw the man on the rock outcrop waving his arms. It was clear to him that they were once passengers on the boat which was now floating around their hull and it made him uneasy. The forty-five-year-old skipper lowered the binoculars and turned to his crew.

'Get in the Zodiac and go bring them in.'

'We're too far out. Can't you get closer?' said Benton, a grizzled man of fifty with leathery skin who had spent more of his life at sea than on land said. He had seen it all, and yet his pale blue eyes glimmered with fear. 'I don't like it out here.'

Carrington didn't like it either, but he couldn't just do nothing. 'I don't like it either, but we have to bring them in safe.'

'We could just call the Coast Guard,' the third crewman said. He was the youngest on the vessel. Stocky and fresh, it was only his second trip.

Carrington considered it, then dismissed the idea. 'We could, but people would ask why we didn't do anything to help when we were so close. People out there might be injured. What if it was you out there, Oxley?'

'I know,' Oxley said, flicking his eyes to the debris field. 'It's just that…Those stories.'

'Old tales; this is reality. There are people who need our help.'

'Maybe those stories are true. I've heard things about this place, too,' Benton said.

'What do you both expect me to do about it? I'll get as close as I can to the shallows, but then you two will have to go out there and pick them up. That's the end of it. Get that zodiac ready.'

Benton and Oxley exchanged glances but knew better than to argue. They set to the task, each keeping a close eye on the water.

They lowered the Zodiac—almost identical to the one used by Nash, Liam, and Tyler; it was fitted with a steel-framed wheel and throttle unit instead of just the outboard motor to control it—into the water, then stepped in. The fibreglass hull a wall of white at their backs, the ocean stretching in every direction.

'Alright,' Benton said, taking charge and moving to the rear of the Zodiac. 'Let's get this done.' He fired up the engine, the motor driving them across the choppy waves. A mile and a half away in deeper waters, the Megalodon sensed the vibrations from the outboard engine and moved to investigate.

***

Tyler knew he was going to die. His face was completely submerged, nose pressed into the rocks as waves lapped over his head. He should have seen it coming. Liam was unstable and couldn't be trusted. Now, his lack of foresight would cost him his life. He was too weak to fight, his exhausted body without the energy needed to fend off the attack. Unlike his attacker, he hadn't eaten to replenish his strength and there was something absurdly funny about it to him in that moment. He would have laughed had his burning lungs not been screaming for air. His hands scrabbled underwater as he desperately searched for something that might help. His hand found a rock, palm-sized, and he picked it up and swung it towards where Liam's hands were holding him underwater. The rock connected with knuckle, and he heard Liam scream and, more importantly, release his grip. Tyler pushed his head out of the water, coughing as he gulped great mouthfuls of air. Liam was coming back at him, knuckles bloody, teeth gritted in anger. For Tyler, there was no thought. The situation had changed. And it would mean he had to attack to save himself. He lurched to his feet and met his would be killer head on.

***

The eighty-foot predator moved through the water, it's immense body gliding with weightless efficiency. It had been stalking a pod of whales for the last four hours when it detected the signal from the Zodiac. The sound was associated with the pain of the explosion when Nash had tried to kill it, and thinking its previous attacker had returned, raced to meet its challenge. Millions of years of evolutionary instinct drove it forward, its body designed by nature to cut through the water with ease as it closed in on the signal. Enraged, and aware its prey was approaching the shallows where it couldn't follow, the creature rose to attack.

***

Benton angled the Zodiac between the waves, the boat bouncing along the surface as it neared the rock outcrop. He was at the rear, sawing at the wheel to try and keep the boat on course.

'It's choppy out here,' Oxley said from the front, shouting to be heard above the engine sound.

'We shouldn't be out here. I don't like it,' the older man shouted back as the wind ruffled his beard. He knew well enough the stories of the waters they were in. He knew of people who claimed to have seen the monster shark that supposedly made its territory there. People he trusted and knew who wouldn't make up fanciful tales. The Devil's Triangle wasn't a place to be. They shouldn't even have been there. They had heard a rumour about a missing boat owned by two brothers and had been hired by their father to search the area and look for them. Ordinarily, it was a job they would have rejected, but a poor fishing season and a broken engine that cost the better part of a hundred and fifty thousand dollars to repair meant that Carrington had to make up as much cash as he could, even if it meant entering the Devil's Triangle. Ordinarily, he would have suggested the family contact the Coast Guard for assistance or the police, but according to the father, one of the missing brothers had recent troubles with the law and he wanted them found privately. Carrington asked no further questions, deciding the less he knew the better, and they had taken the job. Benton liked Carrington a lot, thought he was a good man. But this was one instance where he wished he wasn't so moral and had simply called the Coast Guard to report the survivors after finding the debris. They were fishermen, not a rescue crew. Another couple of hours likely wasn't going to matter to the people on the island either way. On the flipside, he knew the captain really had no choice. He had to perpetrate the rescue. These could well be the people they were looking for and they had been paid to do a job. Benton looked over his shoulder and saw the bigger vessel following them in, keeping as close as it could to avoid running into the shallows. It was as he was looking back that he saw it.

At first, he thought it was a submarine, so immense was the slate-coloured mass that was rising out of the depths. It was only when he saw the six-foot dorsal fin break the surface that he realised what was happening. The fear didn't have time to register, as a split second after the fin broke the surface, the Zodiac was flipped into the air, sending its occupants crashing into the ocean. Benton was the lucky one, as he was thrown off to the side out of the path of the Megalodon. Oxley, however, landed directly in the path of the shark which rose partially on its side, dagger teeth crunching down and extinguishing Oxley's existence before he truly understood what had happened. The water came alive with blood and sent the Megalodon into a frenzy.

***

Carrington saw it happen.

He had just come off the radio to the Coast Guard and arranged for a helicopter to come pick up the survivors when he saw the Megalodon explode from the water. Disbelief was quickly followed by horror as he watched the shark devour Oxley. He throttled back, bringing the boat to a halt and stared at the scene unfolding in front of him. He could see Benton treading water. The shark had gone with its meal, the bloody surface of the water the only sign it had been there. Carrington grabbed the shotgun he kept in the wheelhouse and ensured it was loaded, then headed out on deck.

***

Neither Liam nor Tyler had noticed the attack. They were still fighting, rolling around on the rocks and trying to get an advantage. They separated, staring off under the hot sun. Both men were bloody, and Tyler's eye throbbed and was swelling closed where he had been hit in the scuffle.

'What the hell are you doing? We're saved,' Tyler said, spitting blood onto the rocks. The sun was unbearably hot, his throat dry.

'You were going to take it. My food. He's my father, not yours. You want to feed on him too, don't you?'

Tyler glanced at the rotten, bloated corpse on the ground. 'You're insane. Why would I want that? Just look out there there's a boat it –' Tyler glanced to sea as he said it, noticing how close the boat was to them now. It had stopped in the water, its hull glittering. He also saw the overturned Zodiac and what looked like a man trying to climb onto it. He also saw the blood on the surface of the water and suspected what had happened. Liam looked too, and in that instant, the aggression and tension of the situation dissipated. They both stood and stared at the scene, breathing heavily and drenched in sweat.

'Now do you understand?' Liam said. 'We're never getting off this rock. That thing will never let us.' He turned his back and walked away, sitting cross-legged next to the remains of his father. Tyler didn't understand how he could do that. How he could cope with the smell. He stayed where he was, facing into the wind so he didn't have to handle that stench. He watched the scene on the ocean, hoping rescue would still get to them.

***

The morsel of food hadn't satisfied the Megalodon's perpetual hunger. It circled in seventy feet of water, massive head swaying from side to side as it scanned the ocean for anything else in its territory. It was not used to having its dominance challenged, and as a fiercely territorial creature, it knew only to react with aggression. It returned to the sight of its kill, the bloody water like a homing beacon. It cruised close to the surface, dorsal fin out of the water. Benton sat on the overturned zodiac, numb with disbelief. Even though he believed the stories of the giant shark were true, seeing it was something else entirely. The slate-coloured fin was just twenty feet away. It sliced through the bloody water, then angled towards him. There was nowhere to go, nothing he could do to defend himself. He was going to die and knew it would be a horrific death. A gunshot echoed through the silence. Benton watched as part of the dorsal fin was cut away in an explosion of blood. At first, he was unsure what had happened, then realised it was Carrington. He was standing at the bow, shotgun smoking as he stared at the scene in front of him. Angered by the attack, the Megalodon turned towards the boat and readied itself to attack.

Carrington realised what was happening and sprinted to the wheelhouse, throwing the boat into gear and turning away from the shark, which gave chase, locking on to the churning vibrations from the boat's propellers.

***

'This is our chance. We can get out of here,' Tyler said, for the first time feeling hope and excitement. Liam said nothing. He sat by his father, eating another hunk of rotten flesh.

'What are you waiting for? Come on, the shark is moving off,' Tyler repeated, watching as the man who was sitting on the overturned zodiac slipped into the water and started to drag it towards the island. Tyler knew he had to do something to help and was about to charge into the water when he felt the sting of pain on his back. He spun around to see Liam standing there, scalpel in hand. Tyler touched his back, fingers covered in blood when he looked at them.

'What the fuck?' he grunted as he stared at the younger man, a dishevelled and broken wreck who he no longer recognised. 'You cut me.'

'You can't leave here.'

'What the hell are you talking about?' You're insane. You need your medication. You're sick.'

'I need you. You're still fresh. My father…he doesn't taste so good anymore.'

'Don't you get it? This is our chance. We can both get off this rock and back to civilisation.'

Liam shook his head. 'It's too late for me. You were right. Things can never be normal. Not now.' He slashed out with the blade again, gashing Tyler's forearm. Blood spattered the rocks at his feet as he backed away.

'You can't leave now,' Liam said, flashing a bloody grin. 'You'll bleed in the water and that big fish will come get you. Best you stay here with me and Dad.'

It was then Tyler realised Liam was beyond saving. There was no rational thought, no sanity left. In a way, it made his next decision easier. When every option led to death, there was no reason to fear. Without any hesitation, Tyler lurched into the water and started to swim for the overturned Zodiac.

***

Carrington realised two things in very quick succession. Firstly, that he couldn't possibly outrun the shark, and second, that it was much bigger than he anticipated. His intention had been to lead it out into open water to give Benton time to flip the Zodiac and get to safety, but he knew now that such an option was impossible and would only serve to bring his own life to an end should the shark sink his vessel. Instead, he had started to angle back to the rock outcrop and the shallows. He knew that was his best chance of survival and the best way to use the immense size of the shark to his advantage.

The Megalodon chased its prey, compelled to attack. It increased its pace, angling up from under the stern of the vessel. It accelerated, striking the fibreglass hull just behind the propellers. The vessel lurched out of the water, for a split second its forward momentum slowing as its props spun on fresh air. Carrington was thrown into his instrument panel. Even though his speed control was at maximum, he pushed it harder anyway, using his right hand to steer the vessel. The shallow water warning started to flash on the instruments, and he could once again see the island in front of him. He could also see the Zodiac and Benton pulling it towards the rock outcrop island. Another strike from below caused the vessel to weave in the water. A light started to flash on the instrument panel along with a monotonous alarm sounded as the hull finally gave way and started to take on water. Knowing it was a race against time, he aimed for where the charts said was the shallowest point and hoped he could run the boat aground before it was swallowed by the ocean. Below the surface, the Megalodon moved in for the kill.

***

As Tyler swam to meet the Zodiac, he realised just how tired he was, how drained of energy he had become. It should have been easy, but every stroke was a monumental effort. His back and forearm stung as fresh blood seeped into the water with each stroke, but he had committed too much to turn back now. Even so, he kept waiting for that sting of blade on skin and expected at any time for Liam to grab him from behind and drag him back to the island. He didn't risk glancing behind him, though and knew that every second he was in the water was a second closer to death. He was nearing the Zodiac now and could see an older man in the water trying to flip it over.

'Help me with this,' Benton grunted as Tyler swam closer. 'I can't flip it over by myself.' Tyler reached the overturned inflatable, aware once again how alone and vulnerable he was. He could see Carrington's boat coming towards them and the immense dorsal fin giving chase. The fear gave him a much-needed adrenaline boost, and he and Benton tried to flip the boat over, a task that wasn't as easy as Tyler anticipated. It was difficult to get leverage of a solid enough grip to manipulate the rubber frame.

'Wait, wait,' Benton said. 'We need to do this together. On

three. Ready?'

Tyler nodded, aware that Carrington was bearing down on them at pace.

'Alright, one, two…Three!'

They worked in unison, flipping the Zodiac right side up. Benton tried to pull himself over the edge, but the boat was light, and he almost pulled it back over. 'Dammit,' he said, letting go and treading water. 'You'll have to hold it on the other side until I'm in.'

They were both distracted by the scrape of fibreglass on rock as Carrington ran the ship aground in the shallow water. They watched as the Megalodon hit the rear of the vessel, tipping it onto its side on the rock plateau where it had come to rest. Inside the wheelhouse, Carrington was thrown towards the port window, unable to do anything as the ocean rushed towards him. The windows imploded, the glass shredding his skin. The vessel came to rest, half-filled with water. Carrington swam for air, feet treading water in the capsized cabin. Outside, the Megalodon sensed the blood in the water, and confident it had disabled and wounded its potential meal, moved in to finish it off.

***

Benton pulled Tyler into the Zodiac, both men exhausted as they sat in the small inflatable. They could see the fishing trawler on its side, then watched as the shark circled around it.

'How can it do that?' Tyler said, the adrenaline rush starting to fade. 'We're in the shallows.'

Benton shook his head. 'Shallows here are different. It's not just one landmass but lots of different underground islands spaced out in this area pretty much like the one you were on. Next to impossible to navigate so the whole area is just marked shallow.'

'So there is deep water around it?'

Benton nodded. 'Deep enough. Looks like the captain has run aground on one on of the little islands. Look, the shark is circling the boat.'

Underwater, the Megalodon swam around the rock island, the blood seeping into the water igniting its lust to feed. It scraped its snout against the semi-submerged bow, partially lifting it out of the water then letting it fall back to the rock platform. From his vantage point, Carrington got his first real concept of the scale of the creature and realised that his blood was attracting it. He tried to pull himself out of the water, climbing up the control panels towards the copilot's chair. If he could get there and out of the window directly above him, he knew he would be relatively safe. He scrambled up, trying to haul himself out of the water, but he had damaged his shoulder when the boat capsized, and he couldn't put any weight on it. He was about to try again when he saw a blur of movement a split second before The Megalodon struck the wheelhouse, giant dagger teeth clamping down on the steel frame which groaned in protest. Carrington screamed and flinched away, for a moment finding himself submerged and just a few feet from the immense jaws of the creature. The Megalodon shook its massive head and pounded its body against the rock outcrop. It was only then as the vessel slid forward and scraped against the rocks that Carrington realised what was happening. The Megalodon was trying to pull the boat back into open water.

***

Benton saw it happen and knew exactly what the Megalodon was doing. 'We have to do something to help. Draw it away from the boat.' He moved towards the outboard motor as he said it, checking the frame and control panel.

'No, no engine,' Tyler said, the fear now something impossible to ignore. 'It will come after us.'

'That's what I want; we need to draw it off the captain.'

'It's not safe.'

Benton glared at Tyler as he pulled the chord to fire up the engine. It sputtered but didn't fire up. 'I don't give a shit what you think. We came here to save you and now look what happened. We've already lost one man and I won't let another die. If you don't like it, feel free to get off the damn boat.'

Any further argument was pointless, as the engine spluttered to life. 'Worst case, we can head into that island of yours and wait for the Coast Guard.'

'No,' Tyler said, glancing at the rock mile protruding from the ocean. 'Not back there.'

'Then help me navigate.'

Benton aimed the Zodiac towards the stricken vessel. 'You keep an eye out for that shark,' he shouted above the wind and din of the engine.

'I don't know what we can do to stop it if it decides to come for us,' Tyler shouted back, the fear making him feel sick.

'Trust me on that, I know what to do.'

'And what's that?'

'That wound of yours,' Benton said, nodding at the ugly gash on Tyler's arm which was still dripping blood onto the floor of the Zodiac.

'What about it?'

'Hang it over the side, in the water. Let's see if we can draw our fish in.'

Tyler shook his head. 'No way. I'm not doing that.'

'Do it, or I swear to God, I'll throw you out of this boat and you can fend for yourself.'

That was enough for Tyler. He hung his arm over the side and let his blood drip into the water. At the same time, Benton brought the Zodiac to a stop less than thirty feet from the stricken vessel.

'What now?' Tyler asked, heart thundering as he scanned the water, trying to see through the sun glare.

'Now we wait until he shows.'

***

The Megalodon had pulled the bow of the boat off the edge of the rock platform. It rocked precariously, the wheelhouse filling with water as the ocean threatened to swallow it. Carrington scrambled for something to hold onto, but it was fruitless. He was sure if his shoulder was dislocated or if he had broken his collarbone, and he didn't have enough strength in his functional arm to pull himself to safety.

I'm going to die.

There was no panic in the thought, just an inevitability about the situation. The boat would be pulled into the depths and sink. If he was lucky, he would down before the shark managed to get to him and devour him. It was the photograph that changed his mind. He saw it bob along the surface of the water in front of him. It was his wife and two children. The photograph was sun-faded and one he had forgotten was pinned on the wheelhouse window. The thought of never seeing his family again gave him renewed desire to survive. Carrington used his good arm to try once more to pull himself out of the water, all the time waiting for the jaws to close on him and extinguish his existence. He managed to pull half his body out of the water, the effort making his good arm tremble. He looked down, expecting to see the gaping maw beneath him, but the water was still. The Megalodon was gone.

***

'It's coming right for us,' Tyler said, pulling his arm back into the confines of the Zodiac, not that it would give him much protection when the shark attacked. They both watched the immense dorsal fin slide towards then, one edge bloody and ragged where the shotgun blast had hit it. 'What are you waiting for?' Tyler screamed, backing away from the front of the boat.

'Not yet, just wait,' Benton replied, hand poised over the controls. Tyler couldn't help notice how tacked together it looked. The small A-frame housing the steering wheel and throttle clearly wasn't part of the original design and had been added later. Tyler only hoped there was no water damage from when the Zodiac had been flipped over, and that when Benton decided it was time to take action, everything worked as it should. Any hesitation, any fault would mean certain death. The fin was just twenty feet away now and they could both see the huge body of the Megalodon under the surface. Tyler was frozen, too terrified to speak. It was coming right at them side on. The Megalodon surfaced, jaws gaping, eyes rolling back into its head, ready to kill its prey.

Benton gunned the engine. The Zodiac zipped forward, the Megalodon's jaws crashing down on empty space. Tyler expected Benton to move them away from the giant shark, but instead, he circled back towards it, waited until it started to follow, then changed direction again.

Due to its size, The Megalodon had a slower and larger turning circle than its smaller cousins. Combined with the network of shallow islands surrounded by deeper waters, the advantage it would have in more open waters was significantly reduced. Even so, it was determined not to let the intruder to its territory escape. It gave chase, every time it drew closer to the Zodiac, the Megalodon slowed, having to skirt around one of the island outcrops, increasing the distance between the two. It was the highest stake game of cat and mouse the world had ever seen. Benton kept just enough distance between them, hoping to buy as much time for Carrington as he possibly could. Tyler had realised that the plan was working, and was looking back at the dorsal fin cutting and weaving as it tried to give chase. 'We're doing it. We might well come out of this yet,' he said to Benton, believing for the first time that an option other than death existed. He noticed they were gradually getting closer to the island. He could see Liam watching events unfold. He was about to tell Benton to be careful getting closer, as the water was shallow when a thud from the rear of the Zodiac almost tipped him out of the boat. For a second, he thought the Megalodon had caught up to them and their luck had run out. That, however, wasn't the case. The Zodiac started to slow.

'What are you doing? Speed up,' Tyler said. He stared at Benton and saw fear.

'We lost the engine. Snagged a rock too close to the surface and ripped the propeller straight off. We're stranded.' They both watched as the Megalodon closed in on them.

***

They had come to rest, much like Carrington on a rock plateau. It began just a foot below the waterline. The boat was light enough to stay on the surface of the water and was drifting dangerously close to the deeper waters surrounding the plateau. Benton scrambled to reach under one of the seats and tossed Tyler a paddle. 'Here, you take that side.'

'And paddle out of here? It's impossible.'

Benton scowled at him. 'That's not to paddle out of here; it's to keep us on this rock platform and out of the deep waters.'

The Megalodon circled, lifting its head out of the water and staring at them in the boat, yet knew it couldn't come closer. It rushed the platform, turning away at the last second, sending a wake crashing over the rock plateau and driving the Zodiac away from safety to deeper waters.

'Paddle, paddle now,' Benton screamed.

He didn't need to be told twice. He knew the implications if they drifted into deeper waters. He paddled, using the little energy he had left as the wake washed them perilously close to the edge. The Megalodon swam to the rear of the rock, waiting for them to enter the area where it could get them. Somehow, Benton and Tyler managed to keep within the confines of the shallows. Benton was breathing heavily; Tyler was exhausted. He had nothing left to give.

'Catch your breath,' Benton said. 'He's going to try again.'

They watched as the Megalodon swam away, then came back at them, its speed terrifying. It surfaced and turned away, sending another huge wake rolling towards them.

This time, they were prepared and paddled into it, the Zodiac lurching up over the wave but still being dragged back; this time, they didn't stay within the confines of safety, and were pushed over the edge into the deeper water.

'Paddle, paddle with everything you have,' Benton said, furiously pulling water with the small black paddle.

Tyler followed suit, aware how sluggish he was, how little strength he had left. He was starting to feel dizzy, the lack of food and the trauma of the last few days finally making his body give up the fight. Neither of them dare look but could sense the

Megalodon approaching. A flash of colour from the left and Tyler was sure their luck had run out, but they had done just enough to get back above the shallow rock and out of the reach of the Megalodon. Its jaws snapped down on open water. It lurched away again, soaking them both as it spun away, ready to charge again.

Tyler collapsed onto all fours at the front of the Zodiac. He was done. He couldn't even lift his head.

'Stay with me,' Benton said. 'He's coming around again. You hear me? You have to do this or we're both dead. Pick up that paddle.'

Tyler understood the implications, and desperately wanted to comply, it was just that his body refused to cooperate.

'Come on. Here it comes,' Benton shouted.

Tyler managed to push himself up, the world spinning and lurching. He reached out for the paddle, seeing double and picked it up. He leaned over the side, then dropped it, the paddle bobbing by the side of the Zodiac.

'Here it comes,' Benton said.

Tyler didn't even see it. He felt the boat pushed back, off the safety of their platform, completing a lazy circle as the wake pushed them into open water. He could still see the paddle. It was thirty feet away and drifting in the other direction. Benton realised it was over and tossed his paddle into the bottom of the Zodiac.

'I'm sorry,' Tyler slurred as black spots started to dance in front of his eyes. He was grateful that he would at least pass out before he was devoured. Benton knelt next to him, watching the giant fin come closer and knowing there was no escape. Not now. They closed their eyes and waited for the end.

Nothing happened.

Benton looked around, confused. Tyler saw it too, ignoring the nausea. He watched as the Megalodon raced off towards the rock island.

'Who the hell is that?' Benton said.

Tyler didn't answer. Couldn't answer. He was too exhausted. He could only watch, unsure if what he was seeing was real or an illusion.

***

Liam knew what he had to do. He had asked for a sign and watching the Megalodon's assault had made it clear. He was starting to understand that what he had done was wrong. Even the voice in his head which he had so relied on to guide him was silent and had left him. There was only one thing left that could possibly make things right. Liam dragged his father's bloated corpse towards the water and pulled him in. The corpse floated, the buildup of gases making it naturally buoyant. He waded out, pushing his father ahead of him, knowing this was the only way he would find peace and silence the voices in his head. He went as far as he could walk and stopped. He leaned close and kissed the bloated, blue purple cheek of his father, realising only then that he was crying.

'I'm sorry,' he said, ruffling his father's hair. He watched as the Megalodon charged at the rock outcrop and managed this time to wash the boat into deeper waters. He knew there was no time to waste. He took the scalpel and plunged it into his father stomach, the nauseating stench as trapped gases erupted hardly bothering him. He sliced across the slippery flesh of the gut, pulling open the stomach then flipping the body over onto its front so the rotten contents spilled out into the ocean. When it was done, he took the blade and cut himself, slicing across the same path, mixing hot, fresh blood with the putrid mess in the water before dropping the knife into the water and waited.

The Megalodon was closing in on its prey when it detected the new and incredibly intoxicating signals in the water. Driven by hunger after expending so much energy chasing the Zodiac, it veered off, recognising the putrid smell of flesh as a dead or dying animal and an easy meal. It accelerated, the lust to feed overtaking anything else, even the danger presented by the shallows. Infuriated and determined not to miss another kill, the Megalodon closed on the kill, opening its mammoth jaws wide.

Liam saw it coming and ducked over his father, clutching onto his body as hot darkness engulfed him. He didn't feel any pain as the Megalodon's massive jaws crushed them both in a volatile explosion of blood and bone. The Megalodon's momentum drove it up onto the shallow ledge surrounding the island, almost its entire body coming out of the water. For a moment, it didn't care. It devoured its prize, shaking its mammoth head back and forth as it fed and turning the surrounding water into a bloody froth. Carrington had seen it happen, having swum out through the broken wheelhouse window. He was now at the Zodiac and was pulled onboard by Benton. The three sat there, watching the immense shark thrash, its enormous body becoming more stuck as it struggled.

'Jesus,' Carrington whispered as they drifted back towards the island. Benton paddled, making sure they were clear of the furious animal.

'It's shallow enough to walk here,' Tyler said. They hopped out of the Zodiac and dragged it back on the rock island, a place Tyler never wanted to see again. The trio stood in silence, watching the power or one of nature's most dominant creatures. Out of the water, the scars on its skin were more apparent. A map of the harsh life it had endured.

'He's an old one. He wears a lot of scars,' Benton said.

The comment made Tyler think of Nash, and a wave of sadness swept over him. 'Yeah, he is,' he replied.

They watched as the giant thrashed and then, with a last effort, it rolled off the plateau back into the deep.

Silence.

They stood there, staring at the spot where the shark had been.

'We tell nobody of this. Understand?' Carrington said. 'It would pose too many questions, not to mention damage my reputation beyond repair.'

'What are we supposed to say?' Tyler asked.

'We'll work it out. Just…not yet.'

Nobody argued. None of them had the strength. They remained there in silence until they heard the distant sound of the rescue helicopter approaching. Benton reached into the compartment under the seat of the Zodiac and pulled out the flare gun from the supply box and fired it into the air. They watched the red-orange flare arc into the sky, then the helicopter as it moved towards the island. The rear door opened and a crewman leaned out and gave the thumbs up.

Tyler fell to his knees, weeping uncontrollably.

He was going to live.

He watched as the survival basket was lowered onto the island, lifeguard coming with it, a saviour from the heavens. One by one, they were lifted aboard the waiting chopper. As the rescue helicopter made for the mainland and the hospital, Tyler looked down at the ocean, knowing that somewhere in the dark, a monster roamed.

EPILOGUE

The restaurant was alive with chatter as diners enjoyed their food, a simple thing that Tyler would never take for granted again. It had been six weeks since he had been rescued from the island, and after spending most of that answering questions and giving the authorities the version of events he, Benton, and Carrington had agreed on, he had been allowed to go free. The idea of freedom and travel no longer appealed to him, and so he had returned home. The stranding and subsequent rescue had been covered on the news the world over, and it was attention he didn't like. For a while, after returning home, he remained anonymous, staying in a hotel and trying to figure out what to do next. After a while, he plucked up the courage to call Amy and arrange to meet her.

He waited now in the restaurant, sipping water and wondering what he was supposed to say when she arrived. He was so preoccupied with what he was going to say he didn't notice her come in.

'You've lost weight,' she said.

He blinked and looked up at her. She was the same but different. Different hair. Same perfume. 'I didn't see you come in.'

She took her seat. She looked well, healthy. Better for the time they had spent apart. He started to wonder why he had even arranged this meeting. He sipped his water.

'Off the booze?' she asked.

'I don't drink now. I'm clean.'

She nodded, surprised and a little impressed. 'How have you been?'

'Not too bad since I got back. It's been strange.'

She nodded. The waiter arrived and they ordered their food. Neither of them spoke until he went away.

'You know, I still don't know what happened to you out there,' she said, watching him across the table.

He shrugged. 'It was all blown up by the media. A lot of false stories going around.'

She nodded. 'So, what's the truth? Just between us. What happened?'

He sighed and folded his hands on the table. The tip of the scar where Liam had cut him poked out from under his shirt. He pulled the cuff down to hide it. 'It's like the news said. I'd been hired to help out on a fishing boat, we came across some debris, went to investigate, then ran aground in the shallows. I was the only one who survived. I made it to an island and waited there until I was found by that other boat. They also ran aground on the shallows but managed to call the Coast Guard first. We got picked up and that was the end of it.'

She didn't answer, but he remembered the look she was giving him. She didn't believe him. Seeing that look was like a glimpse into a past and he remembered why he had run away from it.

'I've heard something else. I've heard stories.'

He knew she was waiting for him to prompt her to go on, but he had no intention of doing so. Instead, he sipped more of his water. She went on anyway.

'I heard there was a shark attack. I've heard there were other…incidents. Cannibalism.' She lowered her head as she said it and stared at the tabletop.

He was careful to make no expression even though he screamed inside. He knew well enough the stories. His exhaustion after being rescued had made him delirious. Benton told him later he had been ranting about the shark and flesh eating. Fortunately, by the time he was officially questioned, he was back to his normal self and was able to stick to the story they had devised. Even so, those rumours didn't go away. He didn't think they ever would. He chose his words carefully, knowing of anyone she was most likely to see through any lie. 'It's just stories. People making more of it than there was. I'm here now and fine. That's all that matters.'

'And are you fine. Are you really?'

He opened his mouth to answer but closed it again. Their food had arrived. Amy had a chicken salad. He had steak. He waited until the waiter went away again, grateful for the extra time to compose the lie he was about to say. 'I'm fine. Just…tired.'

'I don't believe you. You're not the same.'

He regretted meeting her now. He knew it was dangerous. Everything was still too fresh. He hoped by meeting her it would rekindle something, but Amy was as much a stranger as she was before he left. 'I can't help what you believe. You're entitled to your opinion,' he said, setting his napkin across his knees.

'The old you would have argued the point. You have changed.' There was a touch of something in the way she said it. Not flirtation as such, not outright anyway, but a sense of testing the waters.

He declined to answer and picked up his cutlery and cut into his steak, hoping that eating would mean less conversation.

He paused and dropped his fork on the plate, causing the other diners to stare.

'What's wrong?' Amy asked, aware that they were being watched. Tyler didn't answer. He simply stared at his plate, the anxiety growing in him by the second.

The waiter appeared, a stalk of a man in a suit that looked too tight to be comfortable. 'Is everything alright, sir?'

'This steak. I asked for it well done. This…this is rare.' He couldn't take his eyes off the blood swimming beside the pink section of meat.

Too close.

Too soon.

Too many memories of a horror he was trying to forget.

'My apologies, sir. It seems there was a mix-up in the kitchen. I'll bring you another at once.'

He lurched to his feet, feeling dizzy, aware that all eyes were on him. 'No, it's alright. I can't eat that. It's your father.'

'Excuse me, sir?' the waiter said, frowning and glancing at Amy. 'I don't understand.'

Tyler blinked and looked at the waiter, then at Amy.

'I'm sorry I just…I'm not ready for this yet.' He dropped the napkin on the table and hurried for the exit, ignoring the whispers and gasps as he hurried towards the door. His mind's eye was filled with flesh, raw flesh putrid with maggots and rot. He knew then what he had suspected all along. He may have lived. He may have survived the ordeal, but part of him a bigger part than he realised had died on that island. It was a part of him he could never get back. Tyler pushed out into the cool night air then broke into a run, weaving around people, dimly aware of Amy calling after him.

He knew he couldn't stop.

He disappeared into the night, soon lost in the crowd.

CHECK OUT OTHER GREAT
DEEP SEA THRILLERS

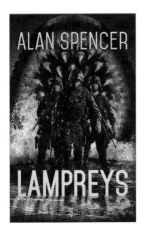

LAMPREYS
by Alan Spencer

A secret government tactical team is sent to perform a clean sweep of a private research installation. Horrible atrocities lurk within the abandoned corridors. Mutated sea creatures with insane killing abilities are waiting to suck the blood and meat from their prey.

Unemployed college professor Conrad Garfield is forced to assist and is soon separated from the team. Alone and afraid, Conrad must use his wits to battle mutated lampreys, infected scientists and go head-to-head with the biggest monstrosity of all.

Can Conrad survive, or will the deadly monsters suck the very life from his body?

DEEP DEVOTION
by M.C. Norris

Rising from the depths, a mind-bending monster unleashes a wave of terror across the American heartland. Kate Browning, a Kansas City EMT confronts her paralyzing fear of water when she traces the source of a deadly parasitic affliction to the Gulf of Mexico. Cooperating with a marine biologist, she travels to Florida in an effort to save the life of one very special patient, but the source of the epidemic happens to be the nest of a terrifying monster, one that last rose from the depths to annihilate the lost continent of Atlantis.

Leviathan, destroyer, devoted lifemate and parent, the abomination is not going to take the extermination of its brood well.

CHECK OUT OTHER GREAT
DEEP SEA THRILLERS

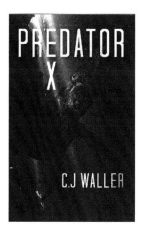

PREDATOR X
by C.J Waller

When deep level oil fracking uncovers a vast subterranean sea, a crack team of cavers and scientists are sent down to investigate. Upon their arrival, they disappear without a trace. A second team, including sedimentologist Dr Megan Stoker, are ordered to seek out Alpha Team and report back their findings. But Alpha team are nowhere to be found – instead, they are faced with something unexpected in the depths. Something ancient. Something huge. Something dangerous. Predator X

DEAD BAIT
by Tim Curran

A husband hell-bent on revenge hunts a Wereshark...A Russian mail order bride with a fishy secret...Crabs with a collective consciousness...A vampire who transforms into a Candiru...Zombie piranha...Bait that will have you crawling out of your skin and more. Drawing on horror, humor with a helping of dark fantasy and a touch of deviance, these 19 contemporary stories pay homage to the monsters that lurk in the murky waters of our imaginations. If you thought it was safe to go back in the water...Think Again!

CHECK OUT OTHER GREAT DEEP SEA THRILLERS

MEGATOOTH
by Viktor Zarkov

When the death rate of sperm whales rises dramatically, a well-respected environmental activist puts together a ragtag team to hit the high seas to investigate the matter. They suspect that the deaths are due to poachers and they are all driven by a need for justice.

Elsewhere, an experimental government vessel is enhancing deep sea mining equipment. They see one of these dead whales up close and personal...and are fairly certain that it wasn't poachers that killed it.

Both of these teams are about to discover that poachers are the least of their worries. There is something hunting the whales...

Something big
Something prehistoric.
Something terrifying.
MEGATOOTH!

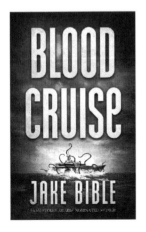

BLOOD CRUISE
by Jake Bible

Ben Clow's plans are set. Drop off kids, pick up girlfriend, head to the marina, and hop on best friend's cruiser for a weekend of fun at sea. But Ben's happy plans are about to be changed by a tentacled horror that lurks beneath the waves.

International crime lords! Deep cover black ops agents! A ravenous, bloodsucking monster! A storm of evil and danger conspire to turn Ben Clow's vacation from a fun ocean getaway into a nightmare of a Blood Cruise!